For Donna Farrell, my Mom
A great mother and friend,
who is missed every day

Cape Breton University Press recognizes the support of the Province of Nova Scotia, through the Department of Tourism, Culture and Heritage and the support received for it publishing program from the Canada Council's Block Grants Program. We are pleased to work in partnership with these bodies to develop and promote our cultural resources.

NOVA SCOTIA
Tourism, Culture and Heritage

Canada Council   Conseil des Arts
for the Arts   du Canada

Cover design by Cathy MacLean Design, Pleasant Bay, NS.
First printed in Canada.

Library and Archives Canada Cataloguing in Publication

Farrell, Susan M. (Susan Maria)
    Basement suite / Susan Farrell.

ISBN 978-1-897009-41-3

    I. Title.

PS8611.A7755B37 2009   C813'.6   C2009-904219-3

Cape Breton University Press
1250 Grand Lake Road
PO Box 5300
Sydney, NS   Canada

Basement Suite

A Novel

Susan Farrell

Cape Breton University Press
Sydney, Nova Scotia

Relationship Survey.

Thank you in advance for volunteering to participate in our graduate work. Transcriptions will be made available on microfiche. You will be provided with your own personal copy. Please answer as honestly as possible and remember once the device is recording, it cannot be turned off so answer all of the questions in a single session. At the end of the recording session, there will be a section to add any comments you feel were not covered; your feedback is welcomed.

You should plan for a six-hour session of uninterrupted time.

1. Self Identification.

Who are you?

<u>Liz:</u>

It's a beautiful day to have a venereal disease.

I am a woman without the capability to have children. I exchanged my procreation for twenty minutes of pleasure that I can't even really remember. It was like the disease itself understood the mediocrity of that event and chose not to announce its symptoms. The disease crept up on me, silently and pervasively invading my body until it surprised me one day and left my uterus a wasteland.

Curable, if only there had been signs. At least, that's what the doctor had said.

"If only there had been signs earlier."

That defines my luck.

I am Eddy's girlfriend, the woman who is dead on the inside.

It's time for a beer.

I am so ready for this relationship survey. I think there's a lot that Eddy and I need to discuss and we never do. We never discuss anything, like we're hoping any problems will go away with time and they do, at least the exact problems disappear but then we're left with these homeless negative feelings. You don't know where they came from but they exist. I couldn't believe it when Eddy said he wanted to participate; normally, he thinks psychological things are stupid, but I think it's just hard for him to talk about his feelings. I've thought about myself a lot over the last several days, ever since we agreed to participate in the relationship survey and I know exactly what I want to say.

Coin-sized ovaries.

I adore sitting in our backyard with all of the flowers, the magnolia trees and elm trees, whenever I want to think. There is something inherently depressing about being underground that makes me feel preserved. Besides, I never got used to the silverfish; they're everywhere. I hate living in a basement, especially in Vancouver; it's dark all the time. There is no light anyway. Why even bother to open the short curtains on the basement window?

Restrained sunlight.

Erotically cold breezes.

Flickering elm leaves.

The crisp bouquet of September flora.

Another abnormally mild Vancouver winter will sing the rains of reflection and the greys of green and I'll still be living underground, earning thirty-four cents above minimum wage, daily explaining to the student loan people that I just can't pay them.

Beer tastes nicer outside.

Now I am a girlfriend but soon I will be a wife, or so that is his expectation. He has given me a week to think about it, but he already knows that we will be getting married in December because it's convenient for his family; they go home each Christmas anyway. Eddy has it mapped out: a few months to save money, get married and spend Christmas with his family, then we have a honeymoon in the spring, at which time I will apparently get pregnant and my woman cycle will be complete. Girlfriend. Wife. Mother. That is Eddy's plan.

I cannot have children.

This is my first photograph for Eddy.

Essence.

No amount of thinking – no matter how proficient or disciplined – will ever lead to an unmitigated intention of your own actions; there will always be contextual levels that others will interpret and thrust upon you as if perhaps you never really knew yourself. As if perhaps someone who had never lived your life might know you better and understand why you did the things you've done. Perhaps they're right but it seems unlikely, although a stranger would never care as much, and through their eyes, they might understand what you never could because in many ways, indifference is objectivity.

It's time to open another wonderful beer.

Eddy proposed to me on vacation although I use the word "proposed" loosely. The moment of proposal should have been the most wonderful moment, but I remember the glorious moment beforehand. That was my moment. When I shut my eyes, I can remember the feeling of having everything I have ever wanted. I never once imagined I would know that feeling. I never once imagined I would recognize that feeling if I was lucky enough to have it. But I did – and I did. Eddy.

Eddy. The love of my life is an arsehole.

Cheers to me. Thank God for the sweet soulful sedation of beer.

"Where should we go for vacation, Wren?" Eddy asked.

"Where do you think?"

That summer was warmer than usual for Vancouver.

"What do you think? You ever been there? Or where do you want to go, Wren?"

"Who's going?" I asked.

"Well, Wren," he said.

He blushed when he said my name and that made my heart race; I fell in love all over again. His eyes twinkled coyly because Eddy already knew where he wanted to go which meant he already knew where we were spending our vacation; he was merely acting like there was a choice. If only he could just say what he wanted right from the start rather than lead me through a suggestive conversation designed to make me reach his conclusion. He bit his lip and shrugged his shoulders as though we were really going to have an open discussion. He was boyish and charming in his white T-shirt and favourite denims.

He had just returned from getting a haircut at the barbershop. Despite the new haircut, he was still wearing too much gel. He was paranoid about his hair getting messy and unkempt.

"Somewhere warm," I said. I guessed he wanted to go somewhere warm – he had purchased a new swimsuit.

"How much debt we got on the credit card?" Eddy asked.

"I thought you paid it off this month," I said.

I have no money.

"I know I asked you to because I had to pay for my hockey thing. Remember? We talked about this. Jesus."

The enchanting thing about leaves is the way they flow back and forth; sometimes, they just tremble while standing still. The leaves are vibrant, bold greens and yet at times, the leaves seem to vanish in a veil of blinding darkness that stays with my eyes long after the image has disappeared. When I close my eyes, I can see the crooked edges of the leaves as they flicker – it's like they're on fire.

It burned me from the inside out.

If I concentrate on that image, the fire becomes real. The fire rages in the hollow of my soul. The scarlet red vehement heat of the Hades flames pricks with a nearness so sincere that dishonesty has sweet appeal. Who wants to succumb to an ugly truth? Not me, not my beer.

"Don't get burned."

"We'll figure that out later," he said with a sigh. "Something warm?"

His hand was smooth to the touch, and when we held on to each other, it was natural. His hand encompassed my hand, and when I slid against his body, my shoulders fell just beneath his; my head fit perfectly into the crook of his neck. Our feet dangled together off the edge of the sofa.

"I think so," I said.

"Those all-inclusive trips to Mexico are still way too expensive for us," Eddy said. He was still smiling. "Where should we travel?"

Your father travels, once a month, for "business."

"You can decide," I said.

"How about the interior?" Eddy asked.

And there it was – the place he wanted all along. Cheap clean fun in your own backyard. Eddy knew a place in the desert climate of the interior, in the Osoyoos, he had a friend who had a friend who had a place, and it was just so warm. Surrounded by mountains. That could be anywhere in British Columbia.

"I think Dakota has a buddy who has a place. I think he's going. We could go camping with Dakota and uh, what's-her-name. What do you think?"

Eddy held my hand when he spoke. His body was hot and inviting and he smelled luscious – like fresh cologne and salon hairspray. He had a vast array of travel brochures for different camping sites in his front pockets. Slipping my hands down the back of his pants for leverage, I pulled the brochures out one at a time with my teeth and he laughed the whole time. He made me giggle and we tickled each other.

The brochures were plain and ordinary; all brilliantly collared with glossy pictures and barely any words. Every place was *exclusive*. Every place was a *secluded getaway* that I would *share with friends*.

Eddy's face was red. His denims were tighter.

"Or... you don't like Dakota all that much, do you, Wren? His other half is real nice, though. He's toned down. Maybe Dakota will actually commit this—"

Eddy never finished that statement.

Dakota was always a tawdry womanizer – it's integral to his sense of self. We both knew Dakota would never be faithful and it was embarrassing to even suggest he might be this time. He knows no other way to be. He has his flashes of humanity – everyone does – perhaps there were more of them when these two men were younger, just boys, when they first developed this friendship bond, but now Dakota's streak of unfounded egoism is undeniable. And his egoism, laced with trendy self-loathing to seem appealing for women with low self-esteem, is based on a fear of actually facing himself.

But Eddy never gives up his obligations; he just isn't that kind of man. If he told Dakota we were vacationing together, then we would be.

Eddy was irrationally desperate to get to the interior. It was a hunger in his eyes. He yearned to see the Canadian desert. The best-kept secret in Canada. He didn't need language to communicate his desire. His whole body convulsed whenever Eddy uttered the words "the interior." It was as though there was *something* there – beckoning to him.

His voice trembled when he mentioned the interior.

Hard.

His face paled and we brushed against each other and downward onto the sofa. His hands slipped beneath my shirt and his lips caressed my neck. His heart was beating fast; there was a pulse against my breasts. All that talk about the interior had excited him. His lips were soft and wet and his hint of stubble tickled my face. He kissed me repeatedly while laughing softly. He gripped my hand once more and kissed each of my knuckles.

"You're so beautiful, Wren," he said. "You don't want to go to the interior, do you?"

"Not really, Eddy. Not with Dakota."

He smiled. But I knew he was crestfallen – his eyes were sad.

The eyes never lie.

That's what Eddy always says.

He chuckles when he says it if there are other people around. A careful gleam forms in his eyes and he casts me a furtive look to reassure – *it's a silly joke, it's humour.* But when we're alone, his words tell a different story. He just doesn't want the words to come back and haunt him.

And that's where I come in. My existence makes him accountable.

The cabin, a one-bedroom log cottage, was on a lake in the interior. This cabin belonged to Eddy's little brother, Dave, and we vacationed with him and Dakota. Apparently, this was a compromise on my behalf – we weren't alone with

Dakota nor were we at Dakota's friend's place – we had the amazing Dave.

The cabin didn't really belong to Eddy's little brother. Dave. It belonged to the extended family of Dave's pregnant girlfriend and several other couples that, in fact, were doing a time-share. Dakota's girlfriend was a different woman by the time we piled into the jeep. It didn't matter – they all blend into one another anyway.

Once we were at the cabin, there were lots of places to go to secure seclusion. Mountains surrounded us. That could be anywhere. I didn't have to spend time with the latest Dakota girl who mistakenly believed she possessed the glorious title *girlfriend*. I abhor hearing them talk about how important they deem themselves to be in Dakota's illustrious life as an artist when they're actually lucky if he remembers their names. I can't bare to hear their "we" talk.

We're so in love. We're made for each other. We're getting married. We just love croutons.

Just a short distance through some heavy fir trees, there was a beach.

The first night we were there, Eddy and I set up our sleeping bags on the beach and had a campfire. We made s'mores, only they weren't real s'mores; we used digestive cookies (the ones with the chocolate coating) and mini-marshmallows because they melt better. The real chocolate cookies melt much better, but who can afford to eat mounds of brown sugar and lard? So, we had diet-friendly s'mores.

It was just the two of us. We wrapped ourselves in the fluffy sleeping bags, gazed at the fire and giggled at whatever we wanted.

Me, my man, and a narrow beach with a view of the purple mountains piercing the sky.

Don't play with fire.

I love the earthy scents of dry driftwood and the beach.

I have two beaches. I have my childhood beach where I learned to swim, where I skipped rocks and played with starfish, not realizing they were alive, and where I broke my arm. And I have my adult beach, where I read romance novels and got sunburns, where I lazed with Eddy, where we baked clams and planned all of our silly little dreams.

You'll get burned.

The fire on the beach was surreal, even iridescent, beneath the jet-black midnight sky in the sheer darkness of the country. Eddy and I, snuggled in our sleeping bags, watched the stars as the fire crackled. Ice-cold beer. We traced constellations with our fingertips.

"You want to have children, Wren?"

I said nothing.

His face.

All good people want to have children. All good people have children. Everyone knows that. You start as a child, you grow up, you go to school, you get a great job, you meet great friends, you fall in love, you have children and then you do it all over again through your children. The alpha and the omega. Everyone knows that – it's the meaning of life.

"I was thinking we'd get married," Eddy said.

Cocking his head to the side so I would know he was serious, he stared at me. He was still waiting for an answer, even though technically he hadn't asked a question. Technically, there was no question.

"That's romantic," I said.

"It's midnight. We're lying on a beach. We're under the stars," he said with a smile.

What causes a human being to want a child? Procreation seems like such a flimsy reason to want to bring another life into this world – to create another human being when every day creation is so stagnant and alienating. Desire can be selfish. Desire can consume.

I tried to laugh a little.

"What do you think, Wren? You, me, kids?"

I remember the look on his face.

Eddy's face had a subtle squarish shape; his jaw was sharply defined. He held his head at a slight tilt because he was in a serious conversation. He wasn't letting me off the hook. I knew when I met this man, he would be the death of me.

We met at a party.

A *fête* in the faddish part of the city. The domicile was filled with students and student wannabes and an exclusive culture of people who fancied themselves *artists*, whether actors, writers, poets, painters, musicians, cartoonists or interior decorators. None of them made a living at it.

The area was in the hip part of the city, Kitsilano, a neighbourhood in Vancouver. It was a village of small apartment buildings with balconies the size of love seats. The remaining houses were divided into one-bedroom suites with windowless rooms. But sometimes, if enough students got together, then they used their massive student loans to afford the whole house.

I had seen everyone before or at least that was how it felt. Attitudes, voices and hairstyles. I was in TV land, predictable plots and secondary characters everywhere and it was all a rerun. I was avoiding some man – he wanted more of whatever he thought he'd found in me but I didn't see him in that way. I just didn't. He was fine; he just wasn't special for me. I wanted someone who made me tingle.

Drinking more beer, I weaved through the crowd with that annoying man following me.

Too many drunken fools looking for fast love.

Then I saw him.

Eddy.

Eddy was perfect, like a black-and-white photo for men's cologne in an art magazine. Lean. Broad shoulders. Short dark brown hair. Slicked back. Brooding. Deep blue eyes with thick black lashes. Sharp jaw line with juicy red lips that cried out: *I pretend I don't need to be understood because it makes me attractive to women with low self-esteem.* His head was slightly tilted to one side for full effect. His denims were low on his waist – his white designer T-shirt was only half-tucked in. His arms were rounded ever so slightly with muscle, but not too much muscle, and he drank his beer directly from the bottle. He looked hungry for life. He made me feel hungry to live.

I wanted to touch him. I wanted to hear him talk until midnight. I wanted to mess his hair. I wanted to feel the heat of his mouth pressed against mine. I wanted to taste his body with my tongue. I wanted to feel the strength of his body against me and in me. I wanted and I wanted.

The man.

I thought if I didn't get to touch him, I might as well stop living. That was what I thought the very first time I laid eyes on him.

Can I pour a beer over your chest and lick it off slowly?

So, I walked over to him.

Taking a long drink, he dribbled some beer over his lower lip and onto his chin. His lips were wet. Moist. Touchable. I placed a serviette to his face and wiped his dribbled beer. He gazed at me with those big blue eyes of his like the embodiment of poetic melancholia.

"You spilled some beer on your chin," I said.

"I know," he said. "I'm real smooth."

He blushed and I fell in love. I had nothing else to do.

"You ever think about kids?"

Autumn is the season of death.

How is that for melodrama?

Some may say that winter is the season of death but everything is already dead in winter. There is no anticipation and fear does not exist for something that has already occurred. Autumn is anticipation – death looms. Autumn is deception. This autumn feels like summer all over again. Soft breezes that caress and lilac aromas that tantalize. But it's finite. I could lie here forever. Now, I wish this would never end.

The beer agrees.

If this would never end, life would always be beautiful. Life would be everything it was supposed to be. Life would be all that I was told it would be. The great promise would be true. Life would be a postcard sent to someone's aunt to tell non-descript stories of the weather on a wonderful vacation. And life would even smell beautiful.

Elm trees.

The leaves smell crisp and invigorating like September mornings when I had to go to elementary school. Everything smelled much better when I was little. Cinnamon sugar on toast. French vanilla ice cream. My mother's talcum powder. Leaves. The rain. My dog. As an adult, none of these things smell quite as good. But the elm trees are almost the same, crisp and pungent, like nuts on the verge of roasting.

When I was little, I used to kick piles of autumn leaves – gold leaves, red leaves and faded brown leaves – beneath my feet and then I would squish them under the weight of my little rubber boots. When I was little, I used to step on the freshly fallen leaves until they had no crinkling power left. That was when I was little. As an adult, I lie in the leaves and drink, digital camera to one side of me and a set of steak knives to the other.

Now the leaves ooze between my naked toes and melt against the last bit of warmth still within my body. The leaves collect in little pools in all the curves my body can possibly offer.

I like it. I like it a lot. It feels good. It feels great. The leaves feel good against my back and thighs; sort of ticklish but not really. It's more sensual. It has impact, feeling, and the comfort of hot cocoa on a cold Sunday afternoon.

Harder. Harder.

Like sex when it was still fresh and new. Sex was so exciting. Sex was *the* agenda. Sex was hours and hours and hours of entertainment. Sex was a throbbing in my vagina that stayed with me long after the act was over. And that felt so good – like he was still with me. Sex was the hunger of the lover. I had no weekends. I had sex. I used to make time for it; clear schedules, skip class, and have a sick day just so I could have a little sex with the man of my dreams. Only I never called it sex. I called it romance.

Romance.

Romance.

It sounds so romantic. Of course, that doesn't explain much. I can't really use the same word to define that same word. But I understand and Lord Byron understands and that's all that matters now.

"What's wrong with vacationing with Dakota?" Eddy asked. "He's my best friend for fuck's sake and it's not like we're rich. Do you want to do something this summer or not?"

I said nothing, as was my usual response.

"I never understand what the fuck you're talking about," he said.

Eddy always made that comment in any kind of argument or discussion; he knew that comment hurt me and would shut me down emotionally. I was paralyzed with every fear, whether trivial or divine, that I have ever experienced in my entire life whenever he said that to me. I could do something but it hurts *twice;* it hurts because it is my Achilles' heel and it hurts because he, the person I love more than anyone, deliberately uses it against me. I never know which hurts more.

"But Eddy, I never said anything weird."

"What you're saying. I just don't *understand.*"

"But I was just talking about vacation this summer—"

"Yeah and that's about as much as I know, sweetheart. Look, that's enough, eh. Whatever you want. Flaws and all, I love you."

"But what didn't you understand?"

"You know how you are. You're a little weird." Then he kissed me and patted my head and the summer vacation had been planned.

"But that's why I love you."

His voice was low and sexy like he was a hero from some Hollywood movie. Staring into my eyes, he gazed a little too long, like perhaps he was wondering whether I knew he was deliberately baiting me. He blushed. And then the hurtful comment becomes just one of many that slips quietly into our history as lovers.

"Love you, Wren."

Not much matters and now there's even less to matter. I see how much goes on without me and I wonder why I ever was at all. We strive our whole lives to attain an affluent degree of boredom: our own encasement, a room with gadgets and pleasure devices, a good fuck to come home to, and small versions of ourselves to live through vicariously when we're too old to enjoy being comfortably bored. What's left when there is no boredom?

It all started with the word romance.

Romance.

I still love the sound of the word. It flows delicately off the tongue like the finest rumba performed between secret lovers at midnight in the light of the moon. Romance is chocolates and flowers and longing looks in his eyes that plead for a single touch. Romance is holding hands with only your fingertips. Romance aches and pulses before it consummates. Romance is for midnight. Romance is for sixteen-year-old Catholic girls, retired men, people who have never felt malice or spite, and of course, the good people who want children. Romance is for so many things and they are all things I will never experience.

Pick up some burgers.

I never did call sex "sex" until much later.

Do you want fries with that?

And then there was that wretched trip to the interior.

Eddy:

I am straight.

I am white.

I am male.

I am Canadian.

I am a straight white male Canadian. I am twenty-eight years old. I am five-foot-eleven, weight 170 pounds. Blue eyes. Short dark brown hair. No distinguishing marks or tattoos. I am a fifth-generation Canadian male of mixed Anglo-Saxon ancestry born unto a white middle-class family with an infrequently practised, yet completely

God-fearing Christian religion. I possess a passionate and strangely conflicting morality that I do not understand yet I am convinced of its truth, and even when confronted with my own religious hypocrisy, I will persevere. I am what everyone wants to be – I am a white man.

Hello, my name is.

From the moment of penetration, it was my destiny. From the moment of conception, it was my birthright. There was nothing to do, nothing to say, nothing to argue, nothing to decide and nothing to deny. The decision was made. The decision was done. The decision is and always shall be. From man to woman, sperm to ovum, my fate was sealed deep within the womb.

***Être*. (To be).** *Sum esse.*

I speak fluently one language only – English – the language of curs. I speak English because I was born in Halifax, famous for its ice-free harbour, the capital city of the province of Nova Scotia in the Maritime region of Canada, located on the eastern seaboard on the Atlantic coast. Predominantly English. Predominantly white. Predominantly mixed Anglo-Saxon heritage. Predominantly liberal. Predominantly from a history of the impoverished and the unwanted. Halifax. Founded in 1749. Founded to spite the French, who had founded Louisbourg in the same province, which was later destroyed.

Nova Scotia was one of the original four provinces, the other three being Ontario, Québec and New Brunswick, to create Canada in 1867. The entire province has only an approximate population of 1 million people and still, it has 21 post-secondary education institutions, most of which are in or near Halifax. Halifax has more bars per capita than any other city in the country of Canada. Some people drink and some do not; most drink.

Warden of the North.

My birthplace was founded by the English to spite the French, who had also founded a place to spite my birthplace, with both sides disingenuously vying for the alliance of the Native American tribes. All of which were later destroyed to avoid the other from having any of it, only to rebuild later if it was something that could be rebuilt. From the rivalry of two men who worked for two other men who created settlements who created cities who created countries who created nations who created history.

My birthplace flourished in its newness with enticing industry that gave birth to unanticipated pains, then my birthplace undeniably declined as modern favours waned, as modern favours are wont to do, leaving behind the earthly scars for future generations. One man gave us industry and fortune and when he was done, he left. The money comes, the money goes.

Self-fulfilling prophecy.

My father was white and his father before him was white and his father before him was white – and so I, too, am white. He was Irish and/or he was Scottish and/or he was English or there's a slight chance he was Dutch or German, but in the end, they produced the ultimate descendant – a straight white English speaking Canadian male or an essential part of the beauteous mosaic that is Canada. And each of these men was born with the Darwinian evolved English tongue – so I too, was born with the evolved English tongue. English: the language that has incorporated all other languages.

Just is a word of un-motivation.

I know how to speak conversational Parisian French, not Québécois French, because French is an official language making its study mandatory in the Nova Scotia school system so we, as a citizenry envisioned by former Prime Minister Pierre Elliot Trudeau, can communicate unreservedly, yet Québécois French is different, and language doesn't equal communication.

I can conjugate the verb "to be." *Je suis. Tu es. Il est. Elle est. Nous sommes. Vous êtes. Ils sont. Elles sont.* It may sound trivial but being is all there is. If you can understand being, then you are that much closer to understanding the journey. Life is a journey, not a destination. To be is always the same and yet to be is always different. No one can see the difference. No one will see the difference. No one will know the difference.

To be.

What I learned in school is useful for trivia, word games, and other leisurely pastimes with my friends. After twelve years of schooling, the verb "to be" is all I can remember. I am. *Je suis.* You are. *Tu es.* He is. *Il est.* She is. *Elle est.* We are. *Nous sommes.* You are. *Vous êtes.* They are. *Ils sont.* They are. *Elles sont.* I learned this verb by studying the basic lives of the Leduc family and their little dog, Pitou. *Mais oui,* they lived a good life, those Leducs. They worried about ants at picnics and fleas on their dog and whether or not they needed to shop at the supermarket for some cheese and some bread. But no matter what happened, the Leducs dealt with the situation together and they dealt with it in the typical Canadian way; with love, understanding, beer and chicken wings, and an insatiable indifference.

And so it goes.

I was born with just enough of every material thing – just enough money, just enough history, just enough language, just enough democracy and of course, the skin – white. I do not need to a specialized phenomenon to be an over-achiever. It is my birthright. I can just sit at home, in my basement suite, and my thousands of blessings will be counted and recorded because I am white and the whole world is mine.

Do not think of me as a human being. Do not think of me as a man. Do not think of me as Canadian. Do not think of me as an individual. I am not a human being. I am not a man. I am not a person. Do not think of me as these things. For I am white.

You know this to be true.

The eyes never lie.

White/*Blanc*/*Blanco*/*Wapék*.

You can smell me before I approach. I smell of untouched snow of the north or fresh blossoms of a tart apple tree. My scent pervades the serenity in the air as I pass you in the street because all that I am and all that I ever will be leaks from deep within the very pores of my pale white flesh. You can feel all of this. You inhale me with every breath you take because I have imbrued every single page of history and the world itself carries the weights of my wonder permeated within in its rocks and soils and waters.

Nothing is untouched. Nothing is untouched.

Every true and great thing I do is inevitable because it is forthcoming in the air around us that never rises and never flows.

Historicism.

History is my falsely honourable and falsely virtuous hero. Flying in a bright red cape with bold blue tights and a big S to symbolize just how special I am, for I am. I am Superman and super am I. Any such history will evince that this much is true. History is my doing and my undoing. History is my any little thing and my every little thing and I am history's little white man. I will never be alone. In life or in death, whether sacred or profane, remembered or forgotten, in truth or in lies, in acknowledgement or in denial, I will never be alone. I am the white man. The world will not forget me. The word will not forget me. The system will not forget me. The individual, as a society, will not forget me. The grave will not deny me.

Straddled across a grave.

Like the multicoloured spectrum of the natural rainbow, I suck in all the colours of humanity and then I am white all over again.

I am the Canadian.

I am so very beyond privileged that it escapes my most basic comprehension, my unbridled dreams, my sexual fantasies and my technological aspirations. I am the export of all exports. I am privileged and I do not even recognize the satiating extent and boundless limits of these privileges and endowments. No matter where I travel – to the small towns dying through dwindling farms or to the sprawling cities infected with desensitized apathy – no matter what I do, I am privileged. I own the whole world – psychological, sociological, economical, educational and environmental – I own the contents lying within, created and being created, and I own the contents yet to be born. They all are mine for my naturalized desires and my unrealized needs and my constipated actions.

I am the Canadian man.

Century after century, I conquered every individual thing and every individual one and now I will conquer myself and not even be aware of the feat.

2. Past history.

What was your life like before your partner?

Eddy:

"Dakota, you fucker, what was that fucking shit you gave me as an answer for the first question? I don't even know what I just said. You fuck. You keep writing shit like that and I'll have to answer this stupid shit myself. Fuck," I say. "Fuck. Damn it. Those fucking sow bugs are behind my toilet!"

"Just spray them, asshole," Dakota says. "Your spray is on the shelf."

"What kind of bullshit are you having me read?"

"Just spray the bugs and get out of the fucking bathroom, man," Dakota says. "We have to discuss your feelings, big boy."

I feel guilty.

You know there's something wrong with your overall drinking habits when you realize you've been standing in front of the fucking toilet for the whole fucking afternoon holding your dick trying to piss. And to make things worse, you're talking into some cheesy two-bit tape recorder unit so you can get paid for it so some other people can go formulate.

Cottony soft and smooth to the touch.

I can stand in the bathroom with my dick in my hand for as long as I want; watching the water in the toilet and in the end, it still ain't going to happen. I can't piss. Although, eventually I start to know why Liz wants to add toilet super-duck or whatever it's called to the list of household cleaning supplies. Toilets can get really fucking dirty. Eventually, I appreciate the new lemon smell of the antiseptic cleaner we use for the bathroom. Lemons are fresh and they smell good.

I can never go when I feel guilty, but I have to piss so badly, I can taste it in the back of my mouth with the beer and the extra hot chicken wings. This beer taste is stronger than that regular shit we usually have because this is freaking homemade shit.

Dakota calls it beer; I call it liquid with alcohol in it. It's his new hobby. Well, I suppose it's my new hobby too; we joined some Grapes-R-Us place in downtown Vancouver. It was next to some place Dakota goes for his lame-ass poetry meetings. We walked inside by accident one day. Dakota hit on the skinny red-haired chick with bulging brown eyes behind the counter so naturally we had to enrol. The place smelled good, like fruit and dry wine, and Liz likes dry wine. Dakota thought we should make beer first.

"Everyone should have a useless hobby."

Dakota has this tongue-in-cheek set of morals that should be used for the average bloke to conduct his life.

Anyone who watches TV can't be all bad.

Everyone is a poem in the making.

No one has to make mistakes.

You don't know where he came up with these rules and you don't really care because they're usually worth a laugh. It's only when you look at him and realize he's wondering why you're laughing, that you think – is this serious for him?

Guilt is a stomachache.

I fucking have to piss so badly.

The toilet looks huge. I have never seen a toilet this huge.

I got my own room when I was maybe ten years old. Before that happened, I shared a room with my older brother Brad. My parents fixed it up with wallpaper of airplanes and trains and other forms of transportation. The room itself was large, but it felt small because Brad took up a lot of room. He wasn't a big kid or nothing like that but he was an ultra moody little shit so he felt fucking huge; like there was an imaginary brick wall surrounding him so he just seemed large. Brad is a waste of a lot of space. You'd know what I meant if you met him. Everyone gets the same feeling when they meet him.

"I thought I wasn't getting my own room until I was thirteen," I said to Ma.

"Your father and I think Bradley needs his own space now," Ma said.

Brad was sitting on the edge of the bed, his arms crossed, staring at the floor. He seemed mad but he had never wanted to share a room with me anyway.

"You're older now, Bradley," Ma said. "You'd like your own room, wouldn't you, Bradley?"

"Whatever," Brad said.

"What did you just say, young man?"

"Nothing, Ma."

"Just take it in the bathroom, young man."

When I did something bad; like curse in front of women or beat up my little brother Dave, my mother would send me to the bathroom. The bathroom was peach coloured: fluffy peach hand towels, peach coloured ducks on the wall, peach-scented soaps. The bathroom was like an orchard in hell. Ma had figured out that we would only play when we went to our rooms: all of our games and shit were in our rooms.

"Aw, Ma."

"We don't use language like that, mister," Ma said. "Now go think in the bathroom."

My mother was eccentric; I used to call her "weird" but Liz said that wasn't respectful. Liz looked at me like I was moose shit. There ain't nothing worse than when Liz looks at you like you're moose shit. Liz can make my dick go limp with her evil look. We can be all hot and heavy and ready to go and then that look – end of party. And then she has the nerve to act all insulted, like maybe she thinks she has no effect.

Weird.

So, Dakota and me had a conversation and we talked about words and came up with eccentric. So, my mother was eccentric. But I swear I never meant nothing by calling her "weird." It's like you can't fucking say dick-shit in this fucking world without some goddamned arsehole calling you a paranoid conspiratorial bigot or woman-hating sexist or an ignorant racist or something fucking bad that takes away your dumb fucker of a useless ass job and then you got no money.

Ultimately, that's all that matters.

You lose your job – end of party.

So the point is, my eccentric little old mother had a different way of doing things. You'd think she never had all those fancy baby books that tell you how to discipline your kids.

"Now that's not nice, ladies don't argue," Cathy said to her dolls in the flowerbed.

Her hair was tied up in pigtails and she was doing the same thing to her little dolls: Lissy and Prissy. They all had stupid names like Missy, Lissy and Prissy. Cathy was playing with them; making up little stories for them, giving them histories and futures. Missy was an orphan and she was going to become the owner of a beautiful country house for orphaned children. It was all so perfect. She was talking to them, telling them they were good little children and that she was going to make them all pretty so they would be successful and people would like them.

"Can I bury them?" I asked her.

Cathy chewed on her lip.

"Can I bury them in the garden with the flowers?"

Still chewing on her lip, Cathy nodded.

I buried all of my sister's dolls in the flower garden in the backyard, among all the tulips and the big orange things that drooped. It was funny. I didn't know why I did it, but I did. At that precise moment, the dolls deserved to be buried.

I pulled the heads off each and every one of those fucking ugly cabbage-headed dolls and then I forked them into an empty spot in the garden and I buried those fuckers real good. I told my sister they were fertilizer that would make the flowers grow better so she let me. You got to let the flowers grow. She sat on the ground and watched. She was crying the whole time but she let me.

Cathy let me.

Ma never quite saw it the same way.

"Go to the bathroom."

"Ma—"

"March."

"Ma—"

"You heard me."

It's okay if they let you.

"Do you know how much your father and I paid for those dolls?"

You don't answer the question because you may not know much but you know enough to know you got to keep your mouth shut. And no, you don't know how much they paid for those dolls.

"Do you realize how expensive those dolls were?"

You don't answer when you're being yelled at.

Ma's voice was high-pitched, a little squeaky, and maybe trembling just a bit. She was rubbing her eyebrows like she might start plucking them accidentally. Her eyes were glossy and bulging; she was scary. I was scared shitless of my mother when she got angry. She never did anything – just sort of trembled. But I could smell a ball of negativity off her and I knew that smell was only there because of me. I did that to my little old mother. And that's what scared me shitless.

"Do you realize, young man?"

Ma's whole body just shuddered. Standing very still, she clenched one hand tightly on her hip, and with the other hand, she rubbed her eyebrow frantically. Then, she stared at me with those big bulging eyes. I hated that part the most. She wasn't doing anything – just staring but I was scared.

Like I might get sucked into the void of bad children.

There is a void and all bad children go there. It's a private place somewhere across the country, somewhere in the streets, or somewhere in the back of your mind. Some kids never realize it's there, some kids visit and some kids never come back. Even an accident or a simple misunderstanding can send a bad kid to the void.

You don't ever want to go to the void, not even for a visit. Brad went to the void; Brad never left the void. You never want to be like Brad. You don't ever want to hear your mother say she wishes you were in the void.

I'm talking to you.

There was never a response to that one either.

"I'm talking to you, young man."

What are you supposed to say? I mean, what the fuck are you supposed to say? I think, at this point in the game you've been caught, you know you're guilty, they know you're guilty, you know you're going to get punished, they know they're going to punish you, you know you're going to say you're sorry, they know you're going to say you're sorry. You know the story, they know the story. Everybody knows everything. What's with all the fucking questions? What else is there to say?

The movie is over. The credits are rolling. Time to buy the soundtrack.

At this fucking point, you're pretty much going to say whatever you fucking can to get out of the goddamn situation. All you know is you're in deep shit and you got to piss. As soon as she sends you to the bathroom, you ain't going to be able to piss because you're going to feel guilty so you have to be convincing to avoid the whole "sending" bit. Sorry ain't working and you can't think of a word that means sorry only with more gusto.

A really big sorry with whipped cream on top.

You got dick all to say. And even they're just staring in silence. Because the whole conversation is already known. You keep saying sorry and they keep saying why. Sorry. Why.

Sorry. Why. Sorry. Why. Sorry. Etc. Etc. Etc. But they're still going to keep you there like maybe they think the response is going to change and then, it happens, the clincher – do you know why you're sorry.

"Why did you do that? Didn't you know your father and I would be angry? Didn't you know this was bad?"

There was never any doubt. You know it's bad. The reason you did it is because you didn't think you'd get caught. Obviously, you're not going to do it if you think you're going to get caught. That's sort of self-defeating but you don't tell your mother you didn't think about getting caught. You definitely know that would be a mistake.

"Do you realize how much we paid for those dolls? Those were your sister's favourite dolls. Look at Cathy. Look at your sister. She's upset. Do you realize you destroyed your sister's favourite dolls? Will you please look at me when I'm talking to you, young man?"

You never look at them. That's the worst thing you can do – you'll get sucked into the void for sure. You don't think they can see you through the haze of anger anyway cause they always keep on ranting. Women rant like it's a sport.

"Young man, listen to me! Young man, are you paying attention? Do you have any concept of money at all?"

I don't remember how old I was.

"What if you had to pay for those dolls yourself?"

"I'm sorry, Ma," I said.

At this point, you would just say sorry over and over again.

Sorry. Sorry. Sorry. Sorry. Sorry. Sorry. Sorry. Sorry.

Like it's some magical fucking elf word that will just make everything right again and it never does yet people still say it all the time; all these adults look like sarcastic fools, and they are, because they know the word sorry cannot make a difference. At least a little kid saying sorry doesn't know the brutal reality yet.

Just leave me alone.

"I'm sorry. I'm sorry. Ma, I'm sorry."

"You look at me when I'm talking to you. Are you listening to me?"

Sorry.

"Go to the bathroom and think about what you've done."

Think about what?

"March, young man."

I think I spent half my life in bathrooms. I was so sorry; I didn't know why I was sorry or what I was sorry for but I knew I was sorry. It was all I could think and all I could say. Sorry. Sorry. God, I can still hear my own voice saying sorry. Sorry. Sorry. Sometimes I dream about it and I wake up in a cold sweat, still muttering sorry for something I did when I was so little, I can't even remember all the details.

Sweat.

"He looked at me funny," Brad said.

"Get in the house, Bradley," Ma said.

Brad never got in trouble.

Brad failed math, science, and pretty much everything. Brad cursed in the house. Brad beat up our dog with my Ma's bamboo collection. Brad broke my mother's glass coffee table. Brad messed up the car every other weekend.

And one fine summer day, Brad beat up the kid across the street so badly he had a total of seventeen stitches in four different locations on his face and neck.

"Yes, Mother," Brad hissed. "He was looking at me funny."

Troy Gillis was blind in one eye.

Brad glared at Ma as he walked defiantly into the house, slamming the door behind him while Ma remained outside to speak with the neighbours about the altercation.

"I'm so sorry," Ma said to Mr. and Mrs. Gillis. I was leaning against the car looking at Troy as he sat in the backseat holding a cloth to his head. He was trying not to cry. The cloth was soaked with blood.

"Scars are cool," I told him.

Troy Gillis was a good guy. He just didn't know how to fight; it was like he always had braces or allergies.

"Don't worry about it, Eleanor," Mr. Gillis said. "We understand."

Ma cried. Mrs. Gillis hugged her.

Not only was Brad never punished for hurting that kid, later in the summer he tore the stitches out.

"I said he was looking at me funny," Brad said when we entered the house. Ma sent me to my room.

That was Brad's reason for everything: they looked at him funny. So Brad failed math because the teacher was looking at him funny and he broke the glass coffee table because his own reflection was looking at him funny and he beat the living shit out of a blind guy.

If you're dumb enough to think a little joke might help him see the light, which I was, and you tell him to get a sense of humour and he tells you to go fuck yourself. That only proved my point: Brad needed a sense of humour. Brad needed a personality, too, but Brad needed so much that you wouldn't know where to begin. It wasn't like you could give him a turtleneck and everything would be better.

You wish you weren't ever related.

"What are you doing, Eddy?" Cathy asked me from the top of the stairwell.

"Stop following me," I said. Both Cathy and Dave used to follow me around: big brother syndrome.

Brad was behind her.

"Go follow him," he muttered. He shoved her down the stairwell.

She screamed as she tumbled, but I rushed upwards and managed to grab her before she fell all the way down.

Brad pushed Cathy down a flight of stairs and mind you, while you might bury your sister's dolls in the garden, you don't push her down a flight of stairs. You can do what you want to her dolls because that's funny. (She laughs at it now.) They were dolls; no one got hurt. It might have been wrong but it was like a normal wrong, because you were a kid and kids do wrong things. When you're a kid, you're just learning, and now you laugh at the little kid things you did.

But no one was laughing when Brad shoved Cathy down the stairs, and now you don't even talk about it. You can only think about what might have happened if you and your other brother hadn't been standing near the base of the steps putting on your sneakers. If you hadn't caught her, then what? If you hadn't seen the fear in her face and the rage in his.

"Bradley!" Ma shouted from the kitchen when she heard the screaming. Dave came running to the stairwell, too.

You thought for sure he was going to get it. You thought for sure there was going to be the look and there was going to be the trembling and then there was going to be a moment when you saw your mother so mad, you wouldn't even recognize her.

With a dishtowel in her hands, Ma walked to the foot of the stairwell and looked at Brad and said:

"Your father will have a word with you when he gets home from work!"

"Fuck you!"

"Bradley!"

With his arms crossed and his legs spread apart, Bradley stood on the top of the stairwell. He looked like the demon child from The Omen. He was sneering. Smacking his lips together, he spit a wad of gum out as far as he could muster down the stairwell toward Ma. It dropped down the stairs and landed in front of my shaking mother. She was shaking but somehow, it was different from her angry shaking.

"I hate him! I hate him! I hate him!" Cathy cried.

"What's wrong with Bradley?" Dave asked.

With sweat on her brow, Ma regained her composure and wiped her hands on her apron. Turning very calmly, she just walked away from the stairwell.

Ma knelt in front of Cathy and checked her over for scrapes and bruises.

You don't say anything because you got nothing to say. You're just waiting for your Da cause he's going to fix it. Or so you think your Da is going to fix it – he fixes everything else and you certainly get in shit when you do something stupid.

"He'll leave when he's old enough."

Da got home.

You weren't supposed to watch them in the kitchen but you did.

"When your mother speaks to you," Da started.

Brad was cursing beneath his breath the whole time just laughing. No matter what Da said, and Da didn't say much, Brad just sat there chewing on his fingers. He drew blood. You couldn't stop watching him because you kept thinking, can't he see the blood? Doesn't he taste the blood? You kept thinking he would stop chewing when he drew blood but he didn't. He never waited for Da to finish whatever malarkey he was spewing – consideration is a favourable trait for young men to have blah blah blah – Brad got up and stormed out.

Ma saw Dave and me watching the big reprimand. Walking over to us, she knelt down and patted us on our heads.

"Your brother had a bad experience," she said.

Altar boys.

So, everyone had to be understanding because poor Brad had a bad experience as a kid growing up. Well, suck my dick. Can I use that too? There's a lot of shit I'd like to do. Let me shove my sister down a flight of stairs. Let me curse bloody blue murder at my mother because I had a bad experience. Let me beat the shit out of the neighbour's kid. Let me rob the general store and get away with it because I had a bad experience. You would never think that's all it takes to justify doing something evil.

No one ever talked about Brad's bad experience.

"What's wrong, Eddy?" Liz asked. She woke me up.

"Just that dream again."

It was a recurring nightmare.

Brad comes home after being gone for so many years only he hasn't changed at all. He's still a little kid with a grimace only he's got this big mother gun and he says it's our fault. He starts shooting people: he shoots Cathy, he shoots Dave, he shoots Da and then he goes after Ma and I try to stop him only he already shot me but I didn't even know. I can't reach Ma because I'm hurt. Ma stands in the doorway to see what the commotion is, she's gaunt and her eyes are dark and hollow.

Susan Farrell

Brad stands there; a man only he's trapped inside his kid body, and he's cursing. He holds the gun. You can hear him pull the trigger and it echoes. Click, click, click. And you see the flash. I can either reach out to my mother and save her or I can grab Brad and stop him. I always reach out to my mother to save her but I never can.

Ma died of cancer.

"It's just the bad experience."

"Are you okay?" Liz asked.

Picking up the blankets, she covered the bed and sat beside me. She cradled me in her arms and let her lips caress my face. She read poetry to me – I had no idea what it was but it sounded nice enough.

She read the longer poems; the older ones that we had to study in school. The poems that tell stories. Her voice was gentle and sweet and the words sounded beautiful coming from her lips – but I never knew what the fuck she was really saying.

It sounded pretty.

Wren.

"What happened?" she asked.

"Nothing," I said.

I slept much better after that but I felt kind of bad because I lied to Liz. The dream was bad that night because, after years of no contact, Brad had called me. He got the number somehow, probably from my Da, and he called me earlier that day. The telephone call didn't bother me. What bothered me was my reaction; I hung up on him.

I never thought I'd do that: a brother is a brother. I don't know why I did that. Da told me he's getting divorced. I don't think he will call again.

I never told Liz. She let me sleep pressed up close against her.

"You're fine, honey, I'm here. Relax."

I don't think I could fall asleep if I didn't have Liz.

It's twenty years later, I'm still in the fucking bathroom, and I still don't know what I'm supposed to be thinking about. Other than thinking about pissing. This is only right since you're in a bathroom and realistically, it shouldn't require a lot of thinking. Why the fuck would you ponder the meaning of life when you're looking at a toilet bowl? Fucking philosophers.

I need to piss but I need to stop thinking about that.

I need my girlfriend. (Don't know where the silly girl is.) She's supposed to be home; she's supposed to be answering this dumb survey somewhere.

I need a raise. (There's a wage freeze at the super-absorbent paper factory.) There's supposed to be an automatic percentage increase every six months.

I need a new car. (The floor fell out of the Volkswagen.) The dealership said they might consider a trade but the car they're willing to give me also looks like shit.

I need a new place. (Not enough sunlight.) Fucking bugs everywhere. There was supposed to be an opening in that new building last month.

I need new hockey gear. (Bruised shins.) My brother Dave was supposed to give me his shit since his girlfriend doesn't want him to play and I can't afford new stuff.

Brad should have gone to Ma's funeral.

I need to piss.

It's starting to get uncomfortable.

Susan Farrell

"What the fuck are you doing in there, man?" Dakota says. "Are you answering the second question or what?"

"Shut up."

Logic.

So, Dakota keeps doing this lame thing to me; he has this "scenario."

"Everyone should have a favourite word." (Dakota's favourite word is "scenario." He picked it up in one of his creative writing classes.)

Picture this. Someone walks up to you (apparently, it don't matter who and it don't matter where you are. That's not the important part). Someone walks up to you and they say: "All dogs are canines. Rex is a dog. Is he a canine?"

What do you say? How do you know they ain't lying to you? What if Rex isn't a dog? What if Rex is the one dog who isn't a canine? Because you got to wonder what kind of a freak walks up to you just anywhere at all and starts spewing off at the mouth about dogs and canines and shit? Someone off their medication, that's who. The government just shouldn't cut Medicare.

You can't answer that question.

He says you can answer it based solely on the information given. I say, what kind of an inexperienced ass bases an answer solely on a few statements? Since when has the whole of life ever been able to be explained solely on a few statements? There's a lot more to truth than language.

Dakota.

Dakota wrote my identity speech for the first question. I didn't really want to do this relationship survey; it's easy cash, and Dakota's better with words than I ever was so it seemed to make sense at the time. He wrote other stuff for me.

Dakota wrote my letter of resignation for the hardware store when he was drunk at the revolving bar overlooking the Vancouver harbour. What kind of a jackass designs a drinking establishment that revolves? Anyway, he had just broken up with some rock-and-roll chick so she would write a love ballad for him. Dakota wrote my resume to the super-absorbent paper factory; he was stoned with the guys and he wrote it on a place mat from Arby's. He had just met his new chick. She was an electrician.

Dakota wrote my last letter to my mother when she was dying with female cancer in the hospital back home. I couldn't write it, I couldn't write that letter at all, so he wrote that letter and he knew what to say for my mother, for me.

The night he wrote my answer to the survey, we were both drunk that night at the 'hoe pub, just off China town, and it was on a napkin.

"Can you remember the colour of the walls?" Dakota asked me.

"What walls?"

"This is a cool bar, white boy, we got to come back. Good waitress."

"I think they're blue," I said.

"I think everything is blue."

"I see a red door and I want to paint it blue."

"That's not funny."

Dakota is one of those guys who got a mother of a scholarship from the government or something to take graduate studies in creative writing and poetry or something like that at some wonderful university with an esteemed program. He has four hours of school a week (and that, apparently, is full time); he sits around a big table with about ten other people and they read what they wrote and say whether or not they like it or whether or not the characters should be wearing red or blue. Apparently, what colour the character wears is of the utmost significance. It's symbolic. Dakota sort of believes it. It's all paid for.

"It's the one good thing about being Native."

"What is?"

"I'm a dollar a word, sweetheart."

"Don't call me sweetheart, Dakota."

"Don't want the world to know your boyfriend is Native? Pucker up. Kiss. Kiss. Love you, Wren."

"Don't even fucking joke, man."

"Sweetheart."

"That's not funny."

"Nothing wrong with being gay," Dakota said.

"If you're gay," I said.

"So I wrote your answer to number one for that relationship shit," Dakota said. "But you know, I think if Liz finds out you got me doing it, you're done. She's already pissed with you, man."

Dakota was always good with words. Putting his round reading glasses on, he stared at me. I didn't know how to explain it to him but I knew there was no way Liz was going to walk away from me.

Usually the reading glasses are reserved for when he's trying to pick up chicks. He's in it for the chicks, but he's good with words. Sometimes I swear that man could do anything with his words.

He speaks like one of them fucking poets.

"I am a fucking poet."

"So, what exactly does that get you?"

"What do I care? It's not like I have to pay for any of it."

Somebody is paying for it.

I don't know what nothing means. And I know that I know nothing and that, I think, makes me a lot smarter than all them shitheads who actually think they know something about how the world works and just how they fit into the great big scheme of things. I'll tell you how you fit into the great big scheme of things: you don't. If you go, there's someone else ready and waiting to take your place. If you don't make and re-make your own place every day that you're alive, you won't have your own place. Why spend a shitload of money to figure out your life ain't worth shit?

"I'm just saying, man," Dakota said. "She hasn't really answered your question yet." Dakota wiggled his fingers like I needed reminding.

Whatever.

Whatever. University. Been there, done that. Been there, done that twice. I still lived at home with my folks; I did the local university both times. Studied biology and chemistry the first time around and totally failed not even halfway through the first term. I didn't even buy the books: great big heavy things. Three of them pay my rent. The books were not even good the next year 'cause they change and update everything so you need to buy the new edition for like an amendment of two paragraphs.

You don't remember going to the university and you don't remember coming back.

Rousseau.

Term two. My Da managed to get me off academic probation cause he remembered there's a date somewhere in the middle of the term and if you withdraw before this date, then there's no penalty. Da did the whole thing. He called his buddy who's now some sort of administrator. They'd been in some union together years ago or something boring like that. Da did it all by himself; my Ma didn't help much. Ma wasn't well then. Da didn't want to upset her; Brad had already run off to some big city somewhere to do God knows what because it wasn't like there were jobs in our lame ass town.

I just remember seeing Ma in the antique chair in the living room, staring out the window, crying and crying.

"I'm cold."

You don't want to upset your mother when she's not well. She's your mother. She has this dream for you 'cause you're her good kid – she sees you in university – she sees you getting a good education and getting a good job. She sees her first-born become a fucked up loser and her daughter gets married unexpectedly and the baby of the family is too young to decide anything. So your Da thinks you ought to re-apply, you re-apply. You go back to university.

Four legs good, two legs bad.

University is the golden dream. University is the diamond mine. University is the key to happiness. University is the goal of all well-adjusted children. Regular people go to university.

Regular people go to university.

They should have it on a fucking billboard or on the side of a bus right next to: **four legs good, two legs bad.**

University will get you everything you've ever wanted and more. Everyone knows that. University is the biggest and most successful marketing campaign ever designed to make money.

A few hundred people watching TV together.

The second time.

The books weren't quite as expensive because I didn't go into the sciences, I went into the arts.

What the fuck do you do with an arts degree? There was some economics and some political science and some electives like fish of the north and magic in poetry or some shit like that; I took them 'cause they didn't start until noon and there was only one paper due. Grace, my first girlfriend, was in one of those classes and I did anything Grace told me to do.

University? Jean Jacques Rousseau: that's the only name I remember. And I can say it the right way too, with a little French drawl.

Bills.

The bills are still coming. The amounts are never the same; the bank people don't keep track of anything and they certainly don't communicate from branch to branch. I used to make payments; I don't bother with them anymore. I didn't even graduate and they send me alumni mail and ask for money.

"Liz," I said. "It's those Student Loan people again. They want to talk to you."

"How do you know it's me they want?" Liz asked. "What if they want you?"

"They asked for you by name."

"Couldn't you tell them I wasn't here?"

"They'll only keep calling. Just tell them you got no money."

"I don't have any money."

"That's why I said to tell them that," I said.

No matter how many times me and Liz move to a new place or a new city even, they can still find us, even though we have to re-apply for all of our identification and shit. All the important things like my boss and my paycheque and all that shit get lost in red tape and bureaucracy but not the student loan police. The student loan police can find us anywhere.

I guess that's why they're so smart, eh.

Don't buy it if you're not going to use it.

Da wanted me to go to university; he wanted me to get opportunities and a high-paying job. I'm making more money at my job than any of my friends who went to university even if they studied something useful. Even Dave had to borrow money from me. (History major. Works as an ESL teacher – which required a certificate.) Dakota won't make half the money I'm making. (Literary major. Currently works at Starbucks.) But I suppose he's a better man than me because he's got a university education. He can quote T. S. Eliot and make Liz blush. I can make Liz blush and I don't need T. S. Eliot.

Harder.

Da sort of paid for the first year and I'm paying him back. Loans were out of the question the first year because apparently my middle-class family made too much money, right? The second year was different because my family was a one-income family. That was the deciding factor: what your parents make. Wren would say a blatant misuse of logic. The two of us are still paying off the debts. She doesn't talk about her debts at all but I can imagine her debts are pretty big.

Humanities 200 - Interdisciplinary Studies.

Wooden chairs with green cushions, tartans stuck to the wall, beer on tap and the College Pub was hard to get a place to sit. Happy hour was every day at three in the afternoon, it lasted until eight, and they had suicide hot chicken wings for ten cents. They served them with lots of sour cream; in these cute little glass dishes shaped like fish. There were pictures of past prime ministers on the wall; someone had drawn a moustache on most of them.

College Pub.

"How long have you been here?" Grace said as she pulled up a chair and sat beside me.

The cold flat plains of the prairies.

My old girlfriend Grace used to meet me in the pub after class. We met up with our friends: Dakota was usually there, half a dozen girls with bad haircuts, and a bunch of guys I didn't really know. They were in either the program with me or in the pub. It didn't really matter. Dakota wasn't writing poetry then. He was studying something else: literature or something.

"Where's Dakota?" Grace asked.

"Well, I thought we'd talk about moving," I said.

Grace laughed at my idea of moving.

Grace had no tits, but I loved her. She was short and everything about her was petite. She wasn't pretty; she was cute. She was always smiling and everybody loved her and they would always give her things: jobs in the university library, gigs at the university radio station, discounts on rent, internships, free beer. She was so nice. She looked like an angel: she had blonde ringlets that she absolutely hated and she would always cut them off and they'd grow right back. She'd just laugh and say it must be her destiny to look like Shirley Temple.

I didn't know who Shirley Temple was.

"She was in all of those movies."

Whatever.

"Oh, yeah."

"The little girl who made everyone smile."

Whatever.

"Right, the little girl."

"Do you know who I'm talking about?"

Whatever.

"Yeah, the little girl. Smiling. Right."

Turn the page.

"Let's head back to my place so we can talk," I said.

Grace had a shape like a sick heron.

Grace laughed. She was always laughing; she had a pretty laugh. She always turned red when she laughed and she was easily embarrassed. She apologized for laughing,

"I'm so sorry, I don't mean to laugh."

Grace was like human ice cream: she was so happy and no matter what shit was happening around you, she could make you feel better. She was a thinker too but I mean she was a real thinker, with things that mattered.

Liz's a thinker, but sometimes I don't know on what planet. When she uses the word "teleological," she loses me.

Grace would never use the word "teleological": she was into real things; she could look at a situation and figure out the best solution and she wouldn't get stressed about it. She had a thick blue note pad of lists. Everything that had to get done and it was organized according to priority. Grace looked after other people's pets, children and grandparents. She timed everything. Everything. Everyone loved Grace. I don't know anyone who never liked her. She was real. She was nice.

"What does nice mean?" Grace asked.

It means I could do better.

"It means you're nice, Grace."

"Can we make this only last for a little bit? I have a test tomorrow."

Grace called sex "this." She never wanted to move; she liked our stagnant home, and all for nice reasons, too.

"I don't know, Eddy, my family is here. My Mom would miss me so much and my sister will need some help with her new baby and who would take my grandmother to the mall? What about your Dad?"

"But there's no work here, Grace."

"But Eddy. Didn't your brother, Brad, say he was trying to start something? He keeps calling you. Call him back to see what he says. He's your brother. I'll support you until the business takes off."

"No Brad."

"Honey."

"I said, no Brad."

"Well, have you thought about getting into social work, like me?"

"Grace, I'm not people-oriented like you."

"I can help you."

Grace would wrap a wound on Satan. Grace was so good herself that it was like she couldn't see the miserable things all around her. She thought everyone was nice like she was. Maybe she was naive but she was nice. Everyone says that about everyone but Grace was so nice.

I never wanted to hurt her; Grace was so soft and cuddly. It was just all part of her never-ending charm. I think that was why I ruined things. How can someone be that fucking good? She made me nervous.

"I have to tell you something, Grace. I have to be honest."

Grace wasn't smiling for long.

"Grace was a complete and utter moron," Dakota said.

The gym, the cheapest gym downtown, was crowded and smelled like chlorine. Dakota never liked my ex but he never said anything about her until we had left that shithole and were safely anonymous in the land of the beautiful people who drink too much caffeine otherwise known as Vancouver. Beautiful British Columbia. AKA Hongcouver.

"You have to wonder about anyone who smiles all the time," Dakota explained. "What is with that? Who smiles all the time? I'll tell you who smiles all the time. Morons smile all the time."

"How do you figure?"

"Misery and tragedy are a normal occurrence within humanity. If you don't notice that, then you're lacking some pretty basic cognitive skills. We can't ignore certain aspects of life because they're unpleasant. I don't know how you put up with her. She was always grinning like an idiot and besides, she had no tits."

Liz has tits.

"Now, Liz is a woman you can be proud of."

"What exactly does that mean?" I asked him.

The weights were too heavy for Dakota but he wouldn't admit it; he wanted to keep up to me. I was going to lessen my load so he wouldn't hurt himself again but sometimes I can't get to the gym, with work, Liz, and hockey, and it looked like this might be the only workout I'd get that week. So, Dakota was really working up a sweat.

"Just that Liz is a fine woman—"

"I would be aware of that," I said and then without thinking I added, "I wouldn't be able to forgive a friend if they slept with her."

A deer caught in headlights.

Getting up from the bench, he flung his towel over his shoulders and wiped his brow. He polished off the last of his water. He put more weights on the bar. The weights slammed into place and the clank hurt my ears.

"Your turn, pal," he said.

Sometimes I think about just how much I don't know and I tell myself:

 I'll go to college. I'll take a course or something. I'll take a course in a subject Liz likes.

I could make her blush the same way Dakota makes her blush. But Liz studied boring shit, all the people she reads change the meanings of all the words they use, and sometimes they even make up new words. Intellectuals think they can get away with anything.

The most for the least.

Right now, I can't see myself making more money than what I'm making at the paper factory. When you luck into a job that pays such a shitload of money, you can't really give it up in good conscience. You got your bread buttered and you even got some fucking jam. Sometimes you think you want a different job but that's just cause you don't really want to work. You want the most for the least.

I mean, I can't see me being able to make more money than this. I can't see any more money than what I'm getting right now. I can't see more money and as much money as this is, there's no way we can afford our own place. What kind of job do you need to buy a house in this dream city? What kind of job do you need to afford a house in Vancouver? Where are these people coming from that they can pay close to a million dollars for a one-bedroom house made of beer glass stucco that leaks in the rain? Are they all in debt? What the fuck is happening?

This is the new middle class.

Liz:

The bathroom door was ajar.

The window was slightly open and the lacy curtain was blowing softly in a breeze. The shower was running and the mirror was a little fogged up. It was not even seven in the morning and my parents were not awake. Uncle Roy was visiting from out of town. He smelled like cigars.

"Liz, honey, could you help your Uncle Roy with something?"

It hurts. It hurts.

Pushing the door aside, I walked into the bathroom.

The day my dog died was the same day I got my period.

It was October. Reluctantly raking mounds of leaves in my backyard, near the Adirondack chairs, I was thinking about Halloween.

"Liz, honey," Mom said. Her voice was the voice of bad news.

The feminine initiation arrived moments after my mother's grim message. I hadn't even finished crying over the dog when the menstrual pain overwhelmed me. There was no way I couldn't focus on it; the pain felt like a thousand small worms writhing and twisting in my lower abdomen. I fell to the ground.

Mom kept shouting at me:

"It's just a dog, for crying out loud!"

But the pain was a fire that demanded attention. The pain was swirling, curling and gripping all of my innards. The pain was beating; stronger and more intense to weaker and bearable. The pain was messy. The pain was large. The pain made me not want to be a woman.

"Your Uncle Roy is arriving today as well, so straighten up," Mom said. "You're not a little girl anymore."

I thought: I fucking hate Uncle Roy.

"I fucking hate Uncle Roy."

And that was the first time I had ever cursed.

My mother, pale, angry and holding a cup of tea, gasped. There was no foul language in our household. We each cursed outside the family abode in front of strangers.

Adults aren't supposed to be naked in front of children.

"It's not fucking fair," I cried.

"Language! Language!" Mom shouted. "I didn't raise you to speak like that! I'll have to tell your father about this."

She was not impressed.

My lips had been so pure and so girlish, so untainted by anything malicious. The word had just appeared in my mind ever so naturally. There had been no conscious effort on my part. It was as if the word had always been there; locked in some obscure corner waiting the most perfect moment to succinctly express my fear and frustration. I started shaking.

Uncle Roy always stayed overnight.

"Go to your room and think about what you just said, Lady Jane."

I never knew who Lady Jane was. As I put the rake away, my mother, teacup in hand, followed along behind me.

"You might as well get used to it," she said. "Women have to deal with a lot of pain, that's what it's like to be a woman. And what's this business about your Uncle Roy? That's my brother you're talking about."

It will be our little secret.

Before she closed my bedroom door, she glanced at me as I sat on the bed holding my gut. I felt dark inside. Sick. I was so angry that women had to go through this once a month; clearly, menstruation was a cruel joke against humanity.

"What are you dressing up as for Halloween?" Mom asked. "Think about that."

I no longer cared about Halloween or my dead pet or even the menstruation; I only cared about another overnight visit from him.

"If you think about something else, you won't notice the pain,"

There was no lock on my bedroom door. My parents slept on the main floor on the other side of the house. My room was on the second floor, with a guest bedroom, my father's home office and a second bathroom. There was no lock on my bedroom door.

Mom was right: thinking about something else did lessen the pain of menstruation.

"I am such a skeptic that I do not doubt the possibility of anything." Thomas Huxley.

I never knew it then but menstruation saved me. I was too old for his tastes. Age is always of the utmost significance for a female. It seems women are never the right age for men for long. Menstruation has always been the focus of my life.

The bedroom door opened and smacked into my dresser. My father, with his cigarette and tea, glanced at the awkwardly placed dresser. Sighing, he put his tea down and shoved the dresser back into place. He leaned against the doorframe. This was the big reprimand. He exhaled.

Lady Jane.

"I heard you're growing up now," my father muttered. There was no eye contact. "That's exciting, eh."

I said nothing.

"Sorry about the dog," he said. "We'll get another one when the time is right."

"I don't want another dog."

What I wanted was to never have a period again. I prayed, literally begged God, to not have this gut-wrenching, painful and messy monstrosity known as menstruation and I also prayed that Uncle Roy would die.

"Hmm," my father muttered. "We'll see how you feel later. Sometimes, feelings change. Oh, and don't curse in front of your mother, she doesn't like that."

My father wasn't big on reprimands.

Drinking his tea, he sighed again. He had to stay a few more minutes so my mother would assume I was receiving a good solid lecture that I would remember for years to come. My father worked in business, some sort of administrative position. I never knew his exact title but sometimes his days were very long and he traveled.

Your father goes away for "business."

"What's this business about Uncle Roy?" my father asked.

"He makes me do stuff," I mumbled. I had never even wanted to say the words. It was as if I had not said them but someone else had. Everything seemed quiet for a very long time as if there was blackness in my head drowning out the world.

"Uncle Roy is a lawyer," my father said. "And you can't be going around saying such things. People can get in trouble. I don't want to hear that talk, is that clear? Is that clear? Girls can't say things like that about men, do you understand?"

My father actually gave a lecture. I understood. It was clear. Girls couldn't say things like that about men. Uncle Roy was a lawyer.

Lighting another cigarette, he rubbed his brow and set his tea on the dresser. He stared at the dresser, stroking it with his hand, for a while before he finally changed subjects:

"Your mother's birthday is coming up, isn't it?"

"Yes," I said.

"Say, Jane," he said. "Can I get you to pick up a card for your mother? I'm going to be out of town for a few days."

"What did you call me?"

My father laughed and called himself old and forgetful. Tossing a few bills on the bed, he finished his cigarette.

" Liz," he corrected. "And you can keep the change."

I thought,

He's paying me to keep quiet.

Every October after that year, my father asked me to purchase gifts for my mother's birthday. Every February – Valentine's Day. Every July – their anniversary. My father was worried he wouldn't be able to choose a romantic card. I had to pick. I even chose all flower arrangements; my mother was always very pleased. I guessed that I had good taste. Or maybe it was because I was the only child; there was no one else he could confide in. It was I or it was no one.

Uncle Roy had four daughters.

The calling of "Lady Jane" was just one more childhood enigma. Whenever I was in trouble, my mother would call me Lady Jane. Even my father took to calling me Lady Jane, eventually, he called me Jane. (I always suspected that he forgot my name.) I knew I was in trouble when I heard the name Lady Jane.

Lady Jane.

Years later, when I studied the brief and endearing life of Lady Jane Grey, I still made no connection. I just thought it was a special name concocted by my mother to indicate discontent.

Eddy.

That night, after my parents went to sleep, Uncle Roy called me disgusting.

The infamous Seahorse, a fixture in Halifax nightlife.

At approximately a quarter to ten on a Friday night, we arrived at the Seahorse, cleverly furnished with backless benches and sawdust covered floors, in the heart of downtown Halifax. I had been living in Halifax for two years. The largest city in all of the Maritime provinces and it doesn't have a tenth of the population of Vancouver. The province of Nova Scotia is not even a third of the size of British Columbia. But being from Cape Breton, it felt large. I had lobster on Thanksgiving. It was an interesting two years.

We arrived just in time for another beer war – a double draft was a buck. Cassie, Colleen, Caitlin and Carrie. The guy friends were showing up later: Scott, Aaron, Mike and Mike. We were like the cast of some badly written teen drama. We had all been friends in my consolidated high school, Scott and Colleen were the only couple, and the whole lot of us had moved to Halifax, each attending different universities and institutions.

The starter city.

"Did you down a beer?" Cassie asked me.

"Nah," I said. "I'm good."

Anyone who could down an entire one in time received free drinks for the rest of the evening. There were many volunteers. There was no hard alcohol, which made things rather easy for the two unsmiling bartenders: Oren (the blonde hairy guy who couldn't laugh) and Frank (the guy with the ponytail who knew he wouldn't be doing this for the rest of his life).

We drank before we went out; we always drank before we went out.

That's the way.

"See anyone cute?" Cassie asked.

"Hey!" Scott said as he arrived.

Cassie, Caitlin and Carrie, in an attempt to be casually rude, sort of walked away. Colleen lingered but never greeted her boyfriend to create an anxious tension, which I was quick to notice.

"Do you want me to go away?" I asked her quietly.

"Not yet," Colleen said.

The three of us stood in the sawdust near a pillar, listening to standard rock music, and scanned the chattering crowd. It felt like we were silent forever.

"You know, you're really hot. You ever think about me in a sexual way?" Scott whispered to me but his whisper, inside the pub, was loud. Colleen heard and stormed away with Scott trailing.

"He's a good guy and all," Aaron said to me as we watched them argue on the other side of the pub. "It's just that – he's slept with all of them except you and my ex. He calls you guys the C plus crowd or vitamin supplements. He's trying to score with all of you. It's just a game for him."

Scott wasn't much to look at; he always wore black but strangely, he never seemed to be one of the kids who wore all black. His hair was always stiff with gel and mousse and he resembled the Ken doll only with darker hair and sideburns. Scott did not look like a player; I was shocked.

Some women can feel ovulation.

"I think you have a right to know," Aaron said. "I hate guys like that."

"That is unbelievable," I said.

"He's an arsehole. Some men are arseholes," Aaron said. "Let me buy you a beer."

Aaron thought it was in my best interest not to sleep with Scott or with anyone who had slept with Scott. Naturally, Aaron and I slept together.

Hello venereal disease.

The sex was so quick and unsatisfying that we actually returned to the pub to continue socializing.

By the time we returned to the Seahorse, Adam, the man wanted by both sexes, was near the pool tables, leaning against the cheap cream coloured plaster wall. He was holding a silver-handled pool cue. His brow was scrunched up with tension and concentration. His eyes were a smouldering black that encased infinity.

Adam had been carved by Michelangelo. He was a dark and delicious angel – radiating as the centre on the hockey team and pondering as the president of the chess club. Adam covered all the bases. Every inch of his sleek body and every single movement and every breath to pass across his lips was the workings of a great masterpiece.

"God, he's so hot," Cassie said.

The others agreed and then they had to talk about it for twenty minutes.

"By the way," Cassie said. "Where did you and Aaron take off to?"

"Grabbed a slice of pizza," I said.

If only that had been true.

His lips were moist.

While they giggled and bantered amongst themselves, I admired Adam in silence. He was a graceful pool player. Precise. Pensive. It took him a long time to decide on a shot. We were several tables away, but I could still see the perspiration on his brow and the hair on his chest was slightly visible at the top of his shirt. If I concentrated, I could hear his low voice calling shots. He took the final shot and won the game.

He seemed to look at me. The others thought he was looking at them; their voices went up an octave. Cassie was certain he was looking at her – she had long blonde hair and blow-me lips. A lot of men looked at her.

Adam had gone to the same high school as we had. We knew his name, we knew he drove a motorcycle and played hockey, we knew he liked REM, race cars, shredded wheat and long-stemmed white roses, we knew that he failed algebra and how he had been suspended for a month, and we knew he took a slut to prom. We knew everything but we had never even met him. Every girl at the Consolidated St. Stephen High School knew Adam.

Putting his pool cue away, Adam leisurely strode between the tables and stood before us.

"Hi there!" everyone was saying.

He extended a hand.

"You're Liz, right?"

"That's me."

Cassie, Colleen, Caitlin and Carrie lost touch with me after that.

"I hear you're applying for a graduate program."

Adam and I barely left each other after that moment. He was a Mi'kmaq, from a reserve just outside Halifax. We moved to the West Coast together, to Vancouver, so he could pursue his art at Emily Carr. Part of our relationship was romance; part of our relationship was necessity. I needed someone and Adam needed to be someone. So we became a loving, giving, supportive couple and he took me to the big city of dreams and opportunities so he could pursue his painting and I could find peace of mind and escape the woes of unemployment or worse still, underemployment.

That plan went swimmingly.

Time for another beer.

Adam stayed with me through everything – when the disease was finally discovered and I had to accept that I would never have children. He was very supportive; he was the most supportive man I was ever with.

Adam.

"I remember my mother being thrown across the kitchen. I remember the sound of her face striking the tiles and I remember seeing the blood bubble in her nose. I remember her crying."

Adam had no pleasant memories of youth.

Standing outside the community centre, Adam told me of his childhood. Our dance lesson, modern and ballroom, started in a few minutes. He needed a cigarette. We were supposed to stand more than thirty feet away from the front entrance. We were the youngest couple there, which always made Adam feel socially awkward. We dressed for the occasion: Adam wore black silk and I wore white. Adam liked me in white.

"Don't you want to talk about your own life?" he asked.

I shrugged my shoulders.

Adam had been playing piano, drinking vodka all day.

Adam put all of his misery and all of his pain into his art. His art was painful to look at and yet, you had to look. And Adam could make anyone feel like the most special person like perhaps no other person of such great worth could ever be born, could ever live, could ever die. Of that, he was certain.

"I'm scared of opening up," Adam said.

Translation: please tell me you want to know me.

I asked all of those personal questions for each and every lover I ever had. It was a customary ritual of the relationship. It was expected. And they told me all their little secrets. And I kept all of their personal treasures.

Adam's whole life was a secret.

Everyone says: I'm not like other people – I can't just open up.

But everyone says that. I've said that. Adam said that. We did the verbal tango for months. As time went on, all of his secrets became my secrets; all of his pain became my pain. All of my strength became his strength. Adam wanted to know my personal demons. Adam wanted to know my soul; he wanted to capture it on canvas and in music. He wanted to preserve my pain for the whole world to see, mounted on a wall, and judged in some public museum.

"Do you want to skip dance class?" I asked.

"I'd like you to talk to me," he said.

"What's to talk about?"

"I don't know. Your childhood. Your family."

"It was normal."

"Tell me that then."

On my eighth birthday, in my family household, we invited neighbourhood kids over and we had ice cream cake. My parents gave me a computer for my birthday gift. On his eighth birthday, his father beat him with a shovel.

It will be our little secret.

If you don't ever talk about something, is it ever true?

I had nothing to say.

When there's nothing to say, there's no point in opening the mouth and wasting oxygen. Open your mouth for something else, friend. Pleasures abound and time is moving on. That was six years and two vastly expensive degrees ago.

Alcohol is the magical key to the soul.

Three shots of tequila and I'm a perfumed ballroom dancer – gaudy white sequins are airborne everywhere. Four shots of tequila and the floor is my best friend. Smooth, shiny, and so close. Who says best friends are hard to find?

Hello Vodka, my old friend. I've come to speak with you again.

Adam tried to continue the serious conversation once the class was over.

"You're so beautiful," he said. "You look good in white."

"You bought it."

"I want to paint you in something white," he said.

"I don't want the attention."

"White is pure."

He had a tirade on the subject; he wanted to paint my naked image in shades of white. He had an entire philosophy based on the purity of white. I was to be the subject of his next art show. I didn't think white was a real colour from a technical perspective.

"White is all colours combined."

He drank before we went out, while we were there and then we would go for a drink afterwards.

It's not that people can't open up; it's that they want to be asked to open up. I am weary of prying. It's all a game. They all want to disclose their little secrets but they want someone to pry. That makes it special somehow. Perhaps it is special.

"I want to know you, Liz. I already know what you've been through; that experience has to be hard for a woman. You can tell me anything."

"I know."

Oh, how I knew.

"Do you love me, Liz?"

Game over.

Love.

And that was the end of that relationship.

When we broke up, about two minutes later, he said I would be the only woman he would ever love. Adam kept his morbid promise. At the time, I never noticed his interests in men but in retrospect, the behaviours seem painfully obvious.

I can only assume I drank more then.

I've never told Eddy that Adam, the gay artist I know, is actually my ex-boyfriend Adam.

Beautiful.

The only thing Eddy has in common with Adam is that they both called me beautiful. You're so beautiful. You're so beautiful. You're so beautiful. Adam said it a lot. Eddy says it a lot. Like maybe neither of them actually cares about me as long as I'm pretty and my breasts are perky.

That's my second photograph for Eddy.

Eddy is not like Adam. He doesn't stand like Adam and he doesn't stare like Adam. He doesn't kiss like Adam, he doesn't play with my hair like Adam, and he doesn't make love like Adam. Eddy doesn't have a glassy look in his eyes and he doesn't let go too soon when he shakes hands. Adam loved my parts like I was art, but he didn't want to touch them. I always felt inadequate because I had breasts and hips and curves; because I was a woman. Eddy is not like Adam.

"I gotta use words when I talk to you." T. S. Eliot.

Eddy doesn't look to be pried and he doesn't try to pry. When we have a commotion of whatever kind – who leaves the stove on, who washes more dishes, whose best friend is an ass – we simply divide to cool down. He'll return with fine silk lingerie in bright colours. He will blush when he returns with these extravagantly prepared gifts (they're always wrapped in shiny papers with ribbons and bows). He'll reach out very bashfully and kiss me on the cheek. He tells me that he loves me with lowered eyes and soft gestures and life continues at a wonderful boring pace. Eddy doesn't even like it when things get dangerously close to a truly revealing moment.

The eyes never lie.

Eddy wants to be that close, he just doesn't want to have to talk about it. It's like he worries that if he says it out loud, it might all disappear. Sometimes, I can see the urgency in his eyes.

There are things I cannot say; he never should have done that half-assed proposal on vacation. I don't want him to stop looking at me the way he does now.

Eddy makes the most of things. He is a magnificent man: lean and sculptured and there's always a certain soulful gleam in his eyes which usually accompanies witty comments. Devilish smiles. He loves to wear white T-shirts and faded denims and he always smells like fresh laundry: slightly warm and like baby powder. Eddy smells good enough to strip and embrace.

The man looks so good, I'm sure he tastes like velvet.

Sometimes when I look at him, I feel soft on the inside. Sometimes we just gaze at each other. His eyes are like the ocean. Sometimes, he'll put on his reading glasses and read entertainment magazines to me with a fake French accent and I'll get so hot for him that I ache with anticipation. I like to watch his shoulders and the shape of his collarbone – his chest heaves slightly. I like to trace the outline of his body with my fingertips and my lips.

Sometimes I think he doesn't realize how he affects me. He asks for reassurance. I tell him I want him because it is all I can manage to say. "I want you...." Want.

Want. vb. Desire for something not possessed; to be without, insufficiently supplied; lacking in a quality or quantity, absent. To require.

Eddy is my Lethe; when I'm with him, I can forget everything that has become the reality of my life. I owe so much money that I will die in debt. I don't have a snowball's chance in hell of ever paying off this debt. Not with this job. You don't see too many employment ads for "Philosopher."

He doesn't grasp the power of the words. I do want him. I ache for him. It's not sexual – that's just the manifestation. I feel him deep within me. A longing. A yearning. My lips start to tingle at the very thought of kissing him, tasting him, feeling the gentle curve of his spine. I love the way his naked body feels when he's hot and sweaty and lying on top of me. He holds me. His voice is throaty.

The French accent is a feat. His voice curls around the words and his tongue gets tied up in his mouth. He's so sweet. Have to kiss him.

"What do you think, eh? Of de nine o'clock, show, eh? Tell me, mademoiselle. Dit moi."

Sometimes, he'll make me wait for it because he's laughing so much. Sometimes, he'll make me say I want it, but I have to respond with a French accent to carry on the game. I can't do the accent the way Eddy can and that makes him laugh. We'll be laughing so hard, we'll be crying. Sometimes, he'll just start peeling off his clothes in these ridiculously exaggerated motions (while still trying to make me laugh with his outrageous accent), as he continues to read about the latest action films coming to a theatre near you. He'll tickle me, and I think he is the best man.

I can't wait to be in Lethe.

3. Employment.

How does your employment impact your relationship?

<u>Liz:</u>

I make thirty-four cents more an hour than the provincially set minimum wage. This was the great job that was available to me in the prosperous West that was not available to me back East. Retail.

I do not have a medical or dental plan per se; I pay approximately fifty dollars a month to the province of British Columbia for the right to see a doctor. If however, that doctor tells me there is something wrong, I am shit out of luck. I have the right to see a doctor but I don't have the right to treatment. Treatment costs. In beautiful British Columbia, I have to pay to learn if I'm dying of cancer whereas in Nova Scotia, at least it's free to discover you're dying. I think I'd rather just die not knowing.

At ten minutes past seven, Eddy hit the snooze button once. Only once. If it's more than once then Eddy says we are lazy. Once means we are treating ourselves to an extra ten minutes.

The Six-Million-Dollar man.

Eddy was awake first; he runs every morning.

After he leapt out of bed, he messed my hair and laughed. He is still amused by the fact that he is a morning person and I am not.

"Wake up," he said.

He did his best Tarzan imitation. Eddy has a secret passion for Tarzan movies; he has watched every film ever made that is related to the legend of Tarzan.

"Don't," I said.

He messed my hair again.

"See you in twenty, Wren."

The pillows felt softer in the morning, like perhaps the fluff needed the weight of a sleeping head to reach its maximum form of comfort. The sheets were toasty warm and the dull sun was barely bright enough to be visible through the curtains on our teeny basement window.

"Why do you always roll over to my side of the bed?" Eddy asked.

"Because it smells like you," I said.

Twenty minutes later, when Eddy returned from his morning run, he was hot, sweaty and totally exhilarated. Even though I was still in my pyjamas and awaiting the coffee, I played the theme from *Rocky* as he entered the apartment.

"Hey!" Eddy laughed.

The tape had been in a bin in a mall sidewalk sale and when I saw it, I thought of Eddy. I had to have it for him. Making whooping sounds, he hopped about the kitchen like a triumphant boxer. He danced around the apartment, laughing and cheering while he took me in his arms and spun me around.

"See what I do for you?" I said.

"You're the greatest, Wren," he said. He couldn't stop smiling. His cheeks were red and rounded. He was laughing.

"Why isn't the toaster working?" Eddy asked. "Did you use the coffee machine and the toaster at the same time?"

"Yes, I forgot."

"We lose that coffee machine your mother gave us, we're not getting another one," Eddy said.

Coffee was such a simple pleasure, though.

"Call me *Rocky*. Is it me, Wren or what?"

Eddy wanted "Rocky" to be his nickname from that point on but it never really stuck. Much to his dismay, the new nickname never caught on and Eddy sulked for perhaps three days.

We have household rules. Rule number one: I never have to answer him before coffee. It's a good rule. Eddy made it – he made most of the rules. He has a set of house rules – he says rules will make our *household* run effortlessly. His eyes flash excitedly when he pores over the rules. He squeezes my hand when he discusses *the household*, which is rule number two.

"The household," Eddy said. "The household is important. If you know the game and the game plan and all the objectives, then there can't be a lot of problems, but more importantly, if there is a problem and problems are to be expected (problems are natural and therefore unavoidable), then you can refer to the house rules and there you have it. Solution. And it's fair because it was a rule that you already knew was there so you can't feel cheated. Life is simple."

"What if we have a situation that isn't covered by the rules?"

"Not possible," Eddy said. His voice was strong and confident and the look of determination in his eyes made me believe. I believed. Eddy was born resourceful: it made him a survivor. Our furniture came from a thrift store operated by a religious group, any new clothes came from a second-hand store, and we didn't eat out except for special occasions. Despite the budget, we did have an alcohol fund although Eddy started making homemade wine and beer.

"We're lucky because you're not one of those females that shops when you get stressed," Eddy said. "Dave is going to have to sell a kidney."

Minimum wage.

Lucy's Vintage Accessories. Corner of Main Street and Fifteenth. Near two major bus routes – one of which goes to the shopping mall with the largest food court in the city. Lucy's Vintage Accessories was a local franchise with three locations in the area. I was scheduled five days a week, seven hours and forty-five minutes, just shy of eight hours to guarantee I did not accidentally receive any overtime.

"I need to return this," she said.

A woman with botched-up bleached blonde hair and a twitch, shook in front of the register. She convulsed a little. Her whole body twitched, and she smelled like cat piss. Once a week, she tried to return some of our merchandise that she had obviously stolen and sometimes, the merchandise was never ours to begin with. We all tried to avoid her but the others were quicker than me. Whenever she argued for her refund, I remember the smile on Eddy's face. His beaming blue eyes, his sarcastic twinge. *"Hey, Wren."* It soothed me. However, the smell of cat piss and rotten eggs brought me back to reality when she spat on me.

"I said," she slurred. One of her fingernails was missing. "That I need to return this."

"You need the receipt to return this item."

The policy was clearly posted on the front door. Big bold black letters on a white background. All capitals. Four inches. The policy was displayed again on the cash register and on a poster near the change rooms. *No receipt – no refund.* In three different languages that were prevalent to the area.

English. Chinese. Punjabi.

"I *lost* it okay, *miss*?" she hissed. "I lost my whole damn purse – my *prescription* – from my doctor – I have uh, *asthma*, you know – and my – my – my – my little baby girl's new clothes – my birth control – *everything* – I got robbed on the bus the other day and *what's* your problem? I'm struggling – *struggling, eh* – to make it in life and this robbery has set me back! You can die from asthma, you know."

Statistically I should be in the high-income bracket.

Lucy's Vintage was not even a large corporation.

"Can't you like just *bend* the rules? You got to give me a break, here, eh? Someone gave you a break. Look at you, *you've* obviously had luck."

One heavy dose of antibiotics and it didn't kill me.

"I'm having like the worst day *ever* alright. And the worst week really and like, o my god! Fuck, I'm going to start *crying*, like this is so *awful*. Are *you* saying you don't *believe* me? *Where* would I get this? Huh? Where? It's *yours*. How would I get it if I didn't just *buy* it? Do I look like a *thief* to you? Haven't *you* ever had a bad week?"

Seven days.

"You *obviously* don't know what *bad* luck is like. You must be real spoilt, huh? What are you? A princess?"

My student loan is $56,000? $84,000? $110,000?

"I'll just get the manager."

"You do that," she muttered with yet another twitch. As I turned, she muttered:

Susan Farrell

"Prissy bitch."

Nina, the eccentric manager of this location of Lucy's Vintage Accessories, was sitting in the back office watching me on the monitor and laughing at my discomfort. Ginger and Noriko were also hiding in the backroom. All three women tried to look busy when I first entered the backroom.

"Hi guys," I said.

Ginger and Noriko smiled sheepishly.

"How's it going out there with Botched-up?" Noriko laughed.

Nina, dressed in her usual bright orange skullcap that smelled of incense, spun around in her office chair and smiled. Her smile said *sagacious*.

She calls me "sugar baby." I don't know why and I don't want to know why.

"How's that man of yours?" she asked.

"Botched-up wants to see you," I said.

"I know the drill," Nina said.

"So, sugar baby, are you going to marry that man of yours, Eddy, or are you going to let him go?"

Marriage leads to children.

"She's stealing something off the counter," Noriko pointed out.

"Okay, okay," Nina said. "I'll handle this. You guys get back to work."

Nina took the botched-up blonde outside, to avoid a scene, or so she said, but the large plate glass window made them look like they were on a flat-screen TV. At first, it appeared a normal conversation with Nina nodding politely as Botched-up twitched. Suddenly, there was a change of pace: Nina, talking with her hands, freaked out on the botched blonde. Flailing arms. Wide eyes. Botched-up blonde cowered.

"That does not look pretty," Noriko said.

"Not so much, no," I said.

Ginger said nothing.

Nina had barely finished with Botched-up when there was another unique customer. This customer wanted us to know how to properly hand out change.

"You're very rude," he said. "You know that? You can't put change down like that. You're unfit to work here. Unfit."

The man nearly spat on me, he was so angry that he was salivating.

Apparently, there is etiquette for change. Change first: small coins to large coins. Give the customer a moment to re-count and put away then count the bills: larger to smaller and then wait for the customer to re-count. He thought we should know this since we are in customer service. Nina told him to get together with last week's etiquette specialist because she thinks bills should be counted first and placed on the counter in front of the customer whereas coins are not to be counted but placed directly into the palm.

Unlike the botched-up blonde, the change etiquette man left the store quickly without further incident.

"Why does everyone think their vision of the world is the right one?" Nina asked. "God, I hate people."

Ginger had little or no idea of what was happening. Ginger was a girly girl, heavily made up with matching accessories. She was easily scared of anything that she has not already seen on TV forty or fifty times so most of our conversations seemed outrageous to her.

"And there's so many of them," Nina said. "Fucking people. They're everywhere."

"I think the bigger question is, who are these people that sit at home and think about how change should be returned. Doesn't that say "psychotic" to you?" Noriko asked. Noriko also hated people. One of her eyebrows was permanently raised into a high arc of perpetual irritation.

"Hmmm."

The change etiquette man had annoyed all of the local businesses that day and his last visit of annoyance was the coffee shop directly across the street from us. We could see him haggling with one of the baristas. For a moment, we watched the charade in silence.

"Does anyone need some extra shifts this week?" Nina said. "I have to do an inventory. And I need a mental health day."

The customers seemed to be proving that a full moon does adversely affect the human personality. One gentleman asked me repeatedly to go home with him; he left the store and returned several times. The word "no" was apparently not in his vocabulary. As Nina kicked him out of the store, Ginger hid in back and Noriko stood by the telephone waiting to call the police. He left without incident but then we were too wound up to deal with anything else that might have happened.

The new shipment of items had already been priced and stocked, the new all-white display was set up in the window, and the paperwork was already underway so Nina made an executive decision. She squeezed my shoulders and told me everything would be all right; she knew about Eddy's proposal but she didn't know about what I had done.

They didn't know Eddy and I had argued this weekend and he had gone away. I was home alone. Eddy was scheduled to arrive home sometime today while I was at work.

"That's it," Nina said. "I'm calling Rob and we're closing up. Let's go for a drink and hear if Liz is going to marry her man or what."

"I don't want to talk about that," I said but I also didn't feel like going home, at least, not yet.

"I'll bet you don't," Nina said. "Let's head out, girls."

The pub was on the same block as the shop so it made sense. Besides, chicken wings were on special and there were five different flavours: volcano, suicide, hot, medium and wimpy. We all ordered medium because that is the metaphor of our lives.

"I hate it when the assholes outnumber the regular people," Nina said.

Nina is filled with homegrown philosophies that she creates from women's magazines, the evening news, the psychic hotlines, various poetry periodicals and black-and-white art house films. Sometimes, when she's had too much lager or when there's nothing better to do in the store, she'll share them all with me.

"Is this based on a proportionate number of individuals who have exhibited such characteristics or is this only a working hypothesis?" Noriko asked.

"It's cute the way you ask questions," Nina said.

"Working hypothesis, sweetheart. I don't deal with anything that's not a working hypothesis. You can always *change* a working hypothesis. You can't change something you deem a reality."

We were duly impressed with that comment, even Ginger said it was an interesting point and she actually joined us in an alcoholic beverage. This was going to be a good night for us. There was a good chance she didn't understand a single word. Her eyes seemed a little too blank;

the pupils were too dilated and the eyebrows were raised too high. She looked like a small child who was at the stage of "why."

She's pretty enough, though.

"You always need an out," Nina explained. "Life is spontaneous by nature. *We* don't like that and sometimes we don't want to *admit* that but if you ever want to accomplish anything, you have to be able to flow. That means accepting changes. You know what I'm talking about, sugar baby."

"Yeah, I suppose I do," I said. You always need an out.

We all laughed. As women, we always laughed when we thought we were getting too serious because as women, we were not supposed to be serious.

It is the way.

You say something serious, you laugh at yourself. You can only say something serious if there is an element of humour because if you actually propose a serious thought, no one will take you seriously anyway. They will tell you to lighten up. They will tell you to smile. But if it seems that perhaps you are joking, the statement might just slip by unnoticed but felt by that deep dark entity known as the subconscious which dwells somewhere within. A woman has to manoeuvre her intelligence.

Just once though, I want to say something and not laugh cute-like afterwards. I want to make a statement. A true statement. I don't want to worry about someone calling me the derogatory term feminist or assuming I'm a fluke or stupid because I have big breasts.

"Shit," Nina said. "I forgot to pay my phone bill."

"Do you think the telephone company has their own police force?" I asked. We were all taking supper together.

The question scared Ginger; she thought it was serious. Panic flashed in her painted blue eyes. Suddenly, we all knew she had forgotten to pay her phone bill, too. Even after we told her it was a joke, she still looked nervous.

"So Liz, when are you going to answer your man's proposal?" Nina asked. Ginger started smiling insanely; the very idea of marriage excited her. Noriko thought Eddy was a disgusting pig and Nina thought things were complicated. And me? Well, it was a little of each: Eddy is a disgusting pig and things are a little complicated.

"He's not going to wait forever," Nina said.

"What about the telephone authorities?" Ginger asked.

I smiled, but on the inside I felt nauseated.

No matter how illogical it seemed, the unpaid phone bill managed to symbolically evolve into every unfinished task in my life and then I knew the phone company would clue into this and certainly cut off the telephone. Eddy would be stressed; he likes the telephone. He phones his sister every other weekend and his father every Sunday.

Family is important.

Besides, I have successfully kept every personal problem, whether it's the lack of a decent pair of dress pumps or my lack of a relationship with my father or the pit my financial problems, from Eddy. He sees me as the perfect voluptuous woman who has no problems, who leads a contented life and who has no wants and no great aspirations. To an extent, it is true. And that it is why it has become true.

Eddy.

"So Ginger, are you still concerned about the telephone authorities?" Nina asked. "Honey, there are no telephone authorities. Okay? But do you think she should marry Eddy?"

"Mmmm, mmm."

Ginger said nothing of value, of course. She smiled and laughed like perhaps there was some big joke happening that we were unaware of (I suspect that she believes we are always telling jokes; she does not want us to think she can not understand). She laughed whenever she thought she heard a punch line. Whenever Ginger laughed, Noriko stiffened in her chair and gave me a secret look.

"Nina is witty," Noriko tried to explain. "Don't you think, Ginger?"

"Mmm, mmm." She laughed politely like a young schoolgirl.

A life-sized Barbie doll.

"Ginger," Nina asked suddenly. (Noriko and I know what to expect. Nina used this tactic frequently). "How about running up to the bar and ordering us another round of beer?"

Ginger, in all her glorious beauty and big blonde curls, jumped to her feet and almost hopped and swayed to the bar. Thirty-six, twenty-four, thirty-six. Rumoured to be the same size as Marilyn Monroe at the height of her career. Bubblegum pink lipstick on big "blow me" lips. Her clothes were ironed perfectly. Her breasts were perky, although they were stationary and her nipples were high on the boob like Colette's so I suspected they were fake. She smelled like expensive salon hair spray but really, there was nothing remarkable about her looks. Her features were pretty but *normal*, not memorable.

I may not be as pretty as her, but I'm too pale and my lips are too thin, that gives me a memorable face.

Ginger never says "yes, but" and I cannot help but wonder if that is why she has never spent a day alone and unadorned in her entire life.

Is that what men want?

"Mmmm, mmm."

"Thanks, Ginger," Nina said. Nina always says thank you.

As soon as Ginger was out of earshot, the real whining started. Ginger was like a burden that we carried upon our shoulders.

"She is so stupid," Noriko said. "And I hate to say that because I'm not a mean person but seriously, I have never met anyone as dumb as her."

Sometimes I think that she is our deepest darkest fear: she is the only woman among us who is married and she does *nothing.* If ever we wanted to marry, we re-think our plans when we see her. Ginger is a shell. She has a teaching license and a lifeguard certificate and golf trophies and she does *nothing.* She is a wife, trying to get pregnant, and she does nothing that he has not already told her to do. He isn't abusive: he is a great man and he treats her wonderfully. He is in love but she has become no one.

"But you'll be just as dumb if you marry that ass," Noriko said. "You can do way better."

Noriko doesn't know what I've done.

"Sometimes two people come together for a reason," Nina said. "Sometimes you need to meet someone to learn something about yourself."

"And what is Ginger learning about herself?" I asked.

Whenever we asked for Ginger's opinion – whether for a display at the shop or what she thinks about the new mayor or how she interprets the latest movie or where we should go for an outing – she had to ask her husband first. She smiles, laughs ever so cutely and then rolls her eyes backwards, almost like she is *surprised* that we would *assume* she had an opinion without him.

"But I'm *married* now!"

You can hear it in her laugh. You can see it in her smile. You feel it in her eyes and as Eddy would say - *the eyes never lie*. Ginger has no opinion unless her husband gives one to her.

Snakes and snails and puppy dog tails.

"Why would she stop doing all of her personal things?" Noriko asked. "That's just creepy."

Noriko was genuinely confused; her brow was furrowed like it always was and she scratched her lower lip repeatedly. "Ginger *is* the embodiment of a void. She wasn't always like that, was she?"

"No," Nina said. "I've known her for years – back when she used to substitute at the elementary school near my home. Ginger was great."

"She has no personality – why would she stop being herself?"

"Because she loves him," I said. "And she has nothing else."

Sugar and spice and everything nice.

The conversation went silent for a moment while we all gazed toward the bar. Ginger, patiently waiting, listened as the bartender explained the nuances of various lagers available on tap.

"Hmm," Nina said. "She does it because she *believes* herself to be nothing. If she loved him, she wouldn't do that. Love doesn't give up and give in. And I'll tell you something else too. He doesn't want or appreciate that. He probably doesn't even know she's doing it – *yet*. One day, however, he's going to look at her and realize she has amalgamated. That's the word, amalgamated. Ginger has amalgamated her own personality into the union that is their marriage and when he realizes she no longer exists, then it all falls apart. He'll feel guilty and she'll feel used. They'll both be *alone*."

"Who isn't alone?" I said.

"Well, aren't you the bitter cookie this evening," Nina told me. "Everyone has these preconceptions about what *men* want and about what *women* want and there is no real difference between the genders. The problem exists when *we,* when all of us, *believe* there is a difference between the genders."

The degrees of truth.

"Are you okay?" Nina asked me suddenly.

I never answered.

Eddy wasn't in the mood for sex that night. Eddy was always in the mood for sex. I was scared. I went to sleep and got up for another great day in retail.

And I remember my old friend *sarcasm.*

"These hats that say 'white only' do they come in red?"

"This shirt says dry clean only. Can I put it in the washer?"

"Can I return this item here that I bought at Super Clothes Mart?"

"This says you're open until nine. Are you open until nine?"

"It's my wife's birthday. Pick something out for her, would you?"

"How much would I have to spend in this store to screw you?"

"I need to use your phone for a long-distance call."

"I want to return this underwear because I've been wearing it and it's too small, but I bought it last year and I don't have a receipt."

"Don't give me any five or ten dollar bills in change. I don't like them."

And then there are the customers who assume you must be stupid if you work in retail but there's a difference between stupidity and low self-esteem.

"I guess you don't need a lot of education to work in this place."

"No, I guess not."

"So I suppose we can't really discuss Dostoyevski while you are wrapping gloves, then, huh? I bet you are not familiar with that name, eh? Ha, ha. You can find his books in a library, dear – we have a library downtown. It's that big building with the pillars. Ask the librarian to help you. Dostoyevski."

You cannot even say his name right.

"No, I guess not."

Can't discuss a Russian novel before noon.

By lunch, every contemptuous customer had become a tightly carved wrinkle in my brow. The headache escalated and every other problem in my life appeared: why the fuck did I study Philosophy? Why the fuck did I have sex with that jackass? Every other problem in my life *escalated*.

By the time the day was over, every muscle, every nerve and every ounce of flesh in my entire body had been run through the spin cycle of some huge washing machine. Or at least, that's how I felt.

Drained. Strained. Pained. Abused. Used. Kicked. Licked. Bitten. Hurt. But for thirty-four cents an hour more than minimum wage, I am expected to endure and smile and always find an *agreeable* solution because the customer is always *right*. I guess that makes me always *wrong*.

Then there was the bus ride home.

2000 people standing in your bathroom.

"Move all the way to the back. We can fit more people on. Move."

2001 people standing in your bathroom.

And when I got home, I just wanted to relax but when I arrived, I found Dakota sitting in the corner chair in my kitchen calling my boyfriend "whipped" and "wimpy" because he was washing the dishes.

"Hey Liz," Dakota said.

Dakota stared at me defiantly: no blinking. He called out in a shrill voice to Eddy while taunting me. Even though he was taunting Eddy, his eyes never wavered from mine. From my swollen toes to the curve in my back to the nape of my neck, I felt a murderous chill. My body went numb.

He knows he can ruin my whole life and he relishes that feeling of power; he likes to know that he could use my naïveté at any moment; my last recourse for happiness could end.

I felt cold.

To undo something.

"We missed you the other night, Liz," Dakota said.

"I went out with some friends," I said.

"Does she make you wear a little maid outfit, too?" Dakota said to Eddy. "Do you have to call her *Madame*?"

"Are you staying for supper, Dakota?" I asked.

"I don't know, Liz," Dakota said. "Do you want me to stay?"

"I've got supper ready," Eddy announced.

"Why don't you run and take her coat, Eddy?"

Dakota is so jealous of Eddy. Not because of me specifically, but because Eddy has *things, adult* things: a relationship, a plan, a life that no longer includes Dakota. Dakota has a slovenly bachelor suite in a frigid concrete building on Granville Street that smells like cereal and incense and a closet filled with empty beer bottles because he's too slothful to return them, yet miserly to toss them out because he wants the refund that's applicable. Dakota is so entwined with his own ego he can't even see what it is he wants. Eddy thinks we should buy a condo in one of the new complexes being built near the harbour. Dakota cannot comprehend such an idea. I've taken his little companion away.

"Let me take your coat, Liz," Dakota said.

I set the groceries on the floor and Dakota took my coat. He hung it up in the closet. He leaned in a little too close as he slid the coat from my arms. His voice sounded loud in my ears.

"If Eddy won't take your coat, I will." He laughed like it was all a joke.

Eddy was chopping vegetables, his focus remained intact. The tension remained tight in my brow and shoulders. Dakota's voice was echoing in my ears along with the rest of my headache.

"Eddy doesn't even know why he's with you."

"We're having pasta salad for supper," Eddy said nonchalantly. He was still chopping vegetables.

"Sounds good," I said.

"Sounds absolutely fabulous," Dakota chirped.

"Eddy takes you for granted."

"How was your day, Wren?" Eddy asked.

"Jesus, you even *sound* like a little fucking married shit. Are the two of you getting married or what?"

I said nothing. I could almost taste the vomit in the back of my mouth.

"You are so wrapped around her finger. Mr. Putty. How can you *stand* without a backbone?"

"Because I'm a fish," Eddy said with a hearty laugh.

"Love comes in *phases*."

"Fine, Eddy, my day was fine," I said quietly. "Thank you for asking. I'm going to take a shower."

They laughed and made comments about me having my period because I seemed to be in a mood. Menstruation is the bane of my existence.

What explains the moodiness of men?

There are days when I don't want Dakota in my home. Those days are growing; he makes me nervous. But I don't want to deprive Eddy of his best friend and I don't want to anger the best friend.

We sat at the kitchen table, we ate our supper, we watched the news on the TV, we made small talk and then the half of my boyfriend that was still single got up and went out to pick up chicks while the other half made tea for after dinner.

Sometimes I wonder which half will prevail. Sometimes. My little Lethe is disappearing.

Eddy:

The day started with orange juice.

Fresh from the trees.

You can't have a day without your certain expected things. Life is all about reliability. Everyone can understand that: you don't even have too say it; it's just understood. You get a good thing going and there's just no reason to change it. Seven a.m. Alarm goes off (it's Liz's crappy radio station she likes to listen to – I'm okay with mornings). It sounds like an annoying buzz with a disco beat. But it's good for Liz, though – she's a freaking tired person in the mornings

Susan Farrell

and if she hears the buzzer or a beeping, it sends her into some sort of nervous shock.

Leaping out of bed, I hit the cold floor with my bare feet and shouted. I forgot how cold the basement floor was. We were supposed to get a cheap rug somewhere.

"Quiet," Liz muttered. "What happened to the snooze? Don't we hit the snooze button in the morning?"

Her eyes were only half open – she was lying on her stomach, peeking out from under the sheets. She was trying not to smile so I messed her hair. She broke down and smiled.

I went for my morning run.

One of these days – running totally buck naked through the streets.

Usually I mess Liz's hair because I can't resist. She's just lying there, mumbling to herself about what she has to do on that day. She doesn't care if I'm listening because she's really talking to herself. She's forgetful and she has to make lists for everything only she usually forgets those too. There are lists all over the basement suite – stuck in books, on shelves, behind vases – there's a shitload of lists tacked to the fridge, hanging on with magnetic fruits and woodland animals. Liz is a little absent-minded but we can't afford to have late charges so the bills need to be paid on time.

A deer in headlights.

The first time you messed her hair, you thought for sure she was going to freak on you.

It was the first time she had ever stayed over at your place.

Everything had gone just right. There was no awkward moment where you look at the person and you try to figure out how you can get out of this. Last night's great idea isn't this morning's great idea. Sometimes, you have the girl stay over your place and when you see she's still in your place in the morning, you sort of think, *Man, you must have been horny last night.* Every inch of your epidermis is telling you that you made a grave mistake.

But everything was okay with Liz – I think it was okay because she didn't act like it was an *event*. She was still sleeping so everything had gone smoothly.

You couldn't have planned it better.

But when you go for a run every morning, you go for a run every morning. If there's a woman in the house, then there's a woman in the house. If she's going to be with you on a regular basis then she may as well know what you're like right from the start. Saves a lot of pain later on in the game. But when you leap out of bed and shout from hitting ice cold tile floor and the woman you're with has a minor heart attack because she's not a morning person, you sort of start thinking about your general plan of how to do things.

"What is it?" she gasped.

She nearly fell out of bed – the sheets were tangled about her waist and she was wearing your T-shirt. Her legs were smooth and pale whenever the sheet slipped and revealed them. She was groping around on the floor looking for her things. She looked like she needed glasses. Her hair kept falling in her face.

"What? Eddy? What is it?" she gasped. "Is there a fire?"

Her eyes were spinning around in her head.

"I run every morning," I told her.

"What?"

"Run."

"Uh, did you want me to go with you?"

"You're welcome. Did you want to...."

"Uh.... Did you want me to? Uh, well, I'm not really a morning person – I could wait – we can have coffee when you get back. Unless you'd rather-"

"That sounds good."

"Okay."

"Okay."

This city in the morning is always grey and on the verge of rain.

White skies.

Then there's semi-clean air and green fir trees and dusty seagulls and bad traffic and grumpy people of every nationality going to work or getting groceries or whatever it is they do on the average day and then I have to piss. It's like every time you go for a run, you have to piss like there's no tomorrow. But no matter what you do, you're not turning around and going back to the bathroom. You know that wouldn't work anyway, because then you'd be too nervous to go.

Then, you'd just be standing there, like you are now, holding your dick in your hand trying to piss and trying to figure out what it is people want you to be thinking about. What I'm thinking about, aside from needing to piss, is why Liz needs time to think about getting married. At first I thought she was just being girly but now I'm thinking, there might be something wrong.

Thinking, without focus, can be a big waste of time. You have to know what you're supposed to be thinking about if you want to get anywhere with it.

"Hey, asshole," Dakota shouts into the bathroom door. "What emotionally charged question are you on now?"

"I don't know."

"Where's Liz?" Dakota asks. "I thought you guys were supposed to be doing this shit together."

"She must be in the bedroom."

During the run, I felt my heart beating, my lungs breathing and then the unwanted heaviness in my bladder. That ruined the run. On the one level, you've got your heart talking to you and your head talking to you and now your bladder. So many organs to contend with.

The bladder just kept hollering out to me:

"Piss. Piss now."

But I couldn't give in. I had to keep running: past all the pale neutral pink stucco houses, past all the school kids in brightly coloured plastic rain coats (how do they make raincoats that tiny?), past all the sleeping dogs that kind of look up when you run by and maybe offer a lazy bark, past everything in the neighbourhood you never really look at. It all looks like the same colour – shades of cardboard beige.

It was a big-city neighbourhood, like the last one you were in and the one before that. Like every other neighbourhood, this neighbourhood had: the grungy laundromat, the fruit market on the corner that also sold fresh-cut flowers and newspapers – the *Calgary Herald*, *Ottawa Citizen*, *Montreal Gazette*, *Halifax Herald*. Chen runs this fruit market that also has weird-looking video games in it and there is karaoke upstairs but I've never gone.

"Morning, Chen, any Maritime papers?"

"Yes, yes, Eddy."

"All right! Thanks, Chen."

"You funny guy, Eddy."

You never figure out why Chen thinks you're a funny guy.

Getting back from the run, Liz was finally out of bed and she was stumbling around in the kitchen. I needed a shower and the shower was a long-deserved reward. I pissed in the shower, too. Why get out?

You should conserve time and energy when you can. You need your little ritual and on the shift days, you got to get all of this done in a certain amount of time. When you're feeling time choking you, you do what you have to do. Sometimes, you got to skip the run and the leaping out of bed for that matter because you're just not in the mood for it. You can use that twenty minutes for finishing off the dream. For snuggling into your girlfriend because she's always warmer than the sheets. For figuring out what you're going to have for lunch. Anything.

"Juice?" Liz asked when I entered the kitchen.

I nodded.

Pouring the juice, Liz sat at the table and sipped on her coffee. I gave her the entertainment section of the newspaper. The juice was always fresh – her parents sent us this juicer thing because they had two. Freshly squeezed juice seemed like a lot of work to me. Liz poured the juice from some great ceramic pitcher she got from her mother (part of a set) and she made the coffee (also from her mother).

If Liz drank her coffee slowly, then she was on her period so I know to expect some moodiness.

Coffee is always referred to as THE coffee because Liz can't seem to function without it. Her face contorts with grumpiness and confusion if she doesn't get her daily dosage. She looks really cute. She'll repeat "coffee" in the conversation until I get her some. *Are we coffee renting a coffee movie this evening coffee? Or do you coffee want to go coffee out?*

I'll be home again, caffeine.

During a break at the paper factory, there was nothing to do. (The factory is not really close to anything, there's only one video game and one newspaper vendor in the staff room, and I read the news in the morning.) I was stuck working with this big guy with a droopy forehead. He almost made it as a hockey player when he was younger. Now he keeps reliving it with anyone who will listen.

"Hey, Eddy, catch the game?"

My team lost.

"As always."

"Don't let it get you down. It looked pretty good for a while. It's only early in the season, if they stick together as a team and really communicate, explain their moves and all, then they can win. It's not over yet. Yeah, they can still win. Just communicate."

Sometimes, more often than not, people don't make any sense. You hear what they're saying, you know what they're saying, and you just have no idea how it fits into what you were talking about. You're talking about hockey and sports and they're talking about potato skins and broken hearts.

Santa Claus. Santa Claus. Santa Claus. Fish. One of these things does not belong.

"*What* are you talking about?" I asked him.

Big Crude. (That's just a nickname and you have no idea what it means but when a grumpy white man is about two hundred pounds heavier than you, you don't ask him a question that may very well be personal and not meant for public knowledge.) He had to fix his glasses and blow his nose. It took him a moment to decide which one he wanted to do first. He decided to explain his sport theory first.

"Pittsburgh, Eddy. There's more to a good hockey game than playing a sport. Right? If Pittsburgh gets it *together*. They can do it. They have all the components of a great team."

This type of discussion is common in the lounge room at work only the names of the teams change according to who is having the conversation and what season it is. Big Crude only discusses sports with us. When it's not hockey season, he doesn't have anything to say. He only discusses Pittsburgh. *Pittsburgh this. Pittsburgh that.* Now, I love hockey just as much as the next guy, but I can admit when my team had a bad game. And they have had bad games. But Big Crude says they don't have *bad* games; they have *unworking components.* You'd think he had a vested interest with the way he prattles on and on about it.

"They are going to win."

"You never know, do you?"

"No. I know all right, they are going to win."

He had a look in his eyes. A look that maybe made him eighteen all over again when those big-city hot-shot coaches first laid eyes on him in the arena. Wearing his skates with the broken laces. He had a broken nose but he was still playing anyway. They were all standing in a line off to the side. One of them was smoking. When he saw them there, he was so certain he was going to make it, he was so certain he was never going to lay eyes on his shitty little coal mining town ever again. He was right – just not the way he wanted to be.

I ditched the hockey conversation and called Liz at her shop on Main Street.

"Hi Liz."

"Hi Eddy!"

"So how's it going?"

"We've only had three customers all morning."

"Yeah?"

"Yeah. How's the factory?"

"Yeah, it's pretty slow here."

"At least it's not raining, Eddy."

"True. True. So, how's uh, Nina doing and the other women there?"

"Fine, I guess. Nina wants to re-do the entire layout of the store. Mostly the front window. She wants everything to be *white*."

"Your day sounds shittier than mine."

"That's the excitement in the store."

"Well, one of the machines broke. We got a guy in to look at it, but he doesn't know what's going on. His wife just left him and he's been whining about that instead of working."

"Eddy, he's in pain."

"Yeah, yeah, I know. It's *tongue-in-cheek*. It's all tongue-in-cheek."

"You're precious."

"What does that mean?"

"It means you're precious."

"I am, aren't I?"

Liz was not home first. Her job is retail and sometimes they need her to stay later. When this happens, you find yourself making supper and you're forced to realize something about your girlfriend: you can cook better than your own girlfriend. You cook like the food's only purpose for existence is to please you. And her. It's all just a skill. Something to learn. She cooks like she's afraid to touch the food – she's scared she's going to ruin everything.

Liz hugs me whenever I make supper.

Dakota dropped in; he had just finished his late afternoon class at university. He's got no one or nothing to do so he eats with us and watches the news before he goes out to prowl. Sunday is the only day he doesn't hang out.

He sat in the kitchen chair in the corner and watched me do whatever it is I'm doing. He had to sit in *the corner*

Susan Farrell

chair because he's a little on the paranoid side. Usually he whistles. He whistles and he whistles. Six days a week, Dakota sits in my corner kitchen chair and whistles – Neil Young tunes. Dakota only knows the chorus of two Neil Young tunes and he doesn't know them well.

"I can't believe you're making supper," Dakota said.

"You know," I said. "I'm going to tell you something my grandfather told me when I was little. He had this friend who used to visit him a great deal. But the man would never say anything. He'd just sit in a rocking chair and whistle. So, if you ain't got nothing to say, go home and whistle in your corner."

"You're whipped," he said.

"Fuck off."

"Look at you! Making pasta salad. What is with this shit? *Pasta salad*? Who even eats pasta salad anymore? Isn't that bad carbs? You could not be any more whipped. Freaking pasta salad."

With snow peas, purple onion and Parmesan.

Sometimes, you make something just to piss him off. That's how it all started. You were just washing some dishes so your girlfriend wouldn't have to do it when she got home and when you heard the ass in the corner calling you *wimpy*, you made the first thing you knew you could make. You can't have anyone telling you what you should or should not be doing. You make the pasta salad because it does bug him. Because deep down you know he'd be making pasta salad for Liz if he could.

So, you make the pasta salad and you discover that you *enjoy* making the pasta salad and you enjoy making the other dishes. Maybe not really enjoy but there's a certain sense of accomplishment and a certain sense of control that you can't exactly deny and that feeling grows when you see the little hushed smile on your girlfriend's face. And it's particularly fun when you realize you've made something better than her – now we have competitive cooking every Sunday evening just before our favourite TV program. You don't even tell a guy like Dakota something like that, especially when he can't even handle the pasta salad.

"You're making pasta salad."

"I'm making pasta salad."

"You're making pasta salad."

"I'm making pasta salad."

Dakota was having a moment of reflection; you know that means he's having a moment. You know you're going to have to be patient with him. He was reflecting on his life and he did not like what he saw. You also know it means he didn't pick up this past weekend or the woman he was after rejected him. He says he doesn't get rejected but Bill and Peter tell me these things. It doesn't happen often, but it does happen. Fucking around is great but at some point, you got to settle down. Sometimes you have to wonder why he doesn't get a girlfriend – a real one. Someone special. You know he wants one, why doesn't he just admit it?

"Are you going to marry Liz?" Dakota asked me.

The chopping knife cracked the counter-top through the onion.

The radio was playing.

She never says she loves me.

It was a question that didn't sound real. You heard it and it made your head ache. You're not really sure if it was said out loud. Because the question was intense. The question was one that maybe you've been thinking about yourself only you can't even admit it to yourself but then when someone else utters the same question – reality docks.

"Why are you so fucking interested?" I asked.

Clearing his throat, he got up and opened the refrigerator. He was looking for snacks or beer, but really he was avoiding me. He cracked open a beer.

"You cheat on her all the time, man," he muttered. "That's all. And she knows and now you've asked her to get married."

He might have made sense.

Dakota dug around in the fridge until he settled on an apple. Returning to his chair in the corner, he munched on the apple.

"Do they still make aprons with bibs?" Dakota asked. "Remember those?"

"I don't know."

"We should check it out at one of those Kitchens and Things stores. I'd like to see if they still have aprons with bibs. Do you remember them?"

"I remember."

When Liz came home, she looked like she was going to pass out. Her eyes glazed over and she went pale. Her mouth sort of dropped open and her legs got all stiff. She stood in the doorway, holding a bag of groceries and a quart of milk. She almost dropped the milk.

"Hey, Mr. Mom, are you going to take your girlfriend's coat or what?" Dakota asked.

Liz looked sick

No one said anything. The kitchen felt quiet. The radio was on but the sound seemed so far away that it offered no comfort from the quiet at all. You could hear the blade chopping through the carrot.

"Are you staying for supper, Dakota?" Liz asked.

"Do you want me to stay, Liz?" he asked.

I didn't want him to stay; he was acting all weird. But he stayed and we had supper and watched the news then we went out for some drinks but Liz stayed in. I asked her to go but she said she wasn't feeling well. I figured it was her period.

I came home early. Liz was sitting at her desk in the bedroom putting on face cream or something. She had just taken a bath and she smelled like strawberries; she still looked a little pale. I'm not really sure but I don't think Liz is happy at the store. She seems to like Nina and the rest of the gang but she's got all those degrees although all you can ever do is teach that shit.

"How are you, Wren?"

"I'm fine."

Liz is always fine.

Silence.

Sitting in front of the mirror, she put her earrings back on and brushed her hair. She watched herself in the mirror and I smiled at her when she noticed me.

"You look beautiful," I said.

She stared deep into her own eyes. Her face was smooth – not a single line hinting of a smile. She was stiff; something was bothering her.

"I love you."

This is the part where you say "I love you, too."

She never said anything.

Not that I need it.

"Shitty day at work?" I asked.

"Yeah," she said. "Did you and Dakota have fun tonight?"

I stroked her hair. Retail can be a bitch; retail is like a giant and diverse complaint bureau. I worked a bit in retail when I first got here before I managed to get my current job. Retail sucks.

"Do you want to watch the stars tonight, Wren?"

"Maybe."

"It's supposed to be a good night to see them. Clear skies and all."

"Yeah?"

"Yeah, I picked up two plastic lawn chairs at the dollar store, too. You want some tea? I made black *currant*. What's a currant? Do you want some tea?"

"Tea's lovely, Eddy. Thank you."

"I'll bring the chairs out. You should put a sweater on, Wren, it's getting nippy. You look cold."

Sometimes you wonder if she's ever going to give that response that's supposed to get echoed back after you tell someone you love them. Sometimes, you wonder why you want to hear that response. But most of the time, you leave well enough alone. Logically, you know if she's still with you, if she's still in your bed in the morning wearing your pyjamas, making your coffee, talking to your Da and your sister every Sunday evening, then something is right. That's logical but unfortunately, you know there's more to life than logic.

"I'll wait for you out back," Liz said.

The tension was almost completely out of her voice. You knew she was towel drying her hair and looking for a sweater – her big white one with the loose collar.

"Yeah. I'll bring the tea outside."

When I finally stumbled outside, her hair was still damp and she was wearing a ball cap. She tried not to look at me. She sat in the chair beside me and was quiet for a while.

"Will you teach me how to play tennis when the weather is nicer?"

"Sure, Wren, tennis is good. Nice competitive sport."

"There's a court near our place."

She was still tense.

You can't expect someone to react with joy and pleasure when they've had a crappy day. You can only hope they'll know that's why they feel crappy. Things always get better. Especially when things are bad and miserable, then you know things are going to get better.

Asshole.

Sometimes, you find yourself thinking about the whole love scenario so much, you end up doing stuff that you shouldn't have done. Something stupid. Something you can't even blame on drinking because you were sober and deep down, you know a drink wouldn't have made a difference anyway. It would have been nice if you could have said you were drunk. But you would have known there was no difference. She would have smelled it off you. You never would have done it if you had given yourself *just a minute* for reflection. But you didn't give yourself that minute.

"What do you mean?" Liz whispered.

Her face was stiff and smooth. Her eyes looked more blue than normal, like they got colder all of a sudden. She was stroking her bare legs. Her calf muscle was flexed. She was staring at me, watching the lines around my eyes and mouth. She was waiting for the punch line. She was waiting for it to be a big joke only it wasn't a joke and there was no punch line.

I was the biggest ass in the entire world, I was getting bigger by the moment, and I just couldn't stop.

Get jealous.

"In the laundry room, just the other day. I didn't want you to think I was keeping secrets from you. What's her name, again? The landlord's wife or girlfriend or whatever she is."

Tell me not to do it.

"And how am I supposed to respond to this?"

"Well, it's not like I was unfaithful."

Get jealous.

"I see."

That was all she said.

And you know you only did it because you wanted a reaction. You know you only told her because you wanted a reaction. You didn't plan it that way but when you finally gave yourself *that minute*, you knew the truth. You wanted – you didn't even *want* – you *needed* to hear her say something. And when you realized you needed something well, that was a whole different ball game.

Liz.

Yeah maybe that did bother her more than I thought. At the time, I never really thought she was mad at me.

4. Socialization patterns.

What are your social circles like and how, if at all, do they impact your relationship?

Eddy:

Dakota is not his real name, it's his legal name now, and it was a nickname when we were younger.

"Get the fuck out of the bathroom, man," Dakota says.

Dakota is my closest friend; we've known each other since we were twelve, since his father died and his mother moved into the house on the corner of my street. As soon as he was accepted into university on a scholarship, he applied for a legal name change. He figured Dakota would get him laid and as far as I can tell, it's been working although he is pretty smooth to start with, cool name or no cool name.

Keep your head down.

Maybe I should have written that identity speech – the answer for the first question – it wasn't mine. Dakota wrote it. I mean, you are who you are. Why think about it? Can you ask a question any more retarded than that? I couldn't answer that question. You want to know who I am? Then sit down with me and get to know me like a real human being.

Speeches, toasts, and any sort of public things are rarely mine. I'm not real good with formal shit like that. I say it like it is. Plain and simple. Whenever I need to say something and have it mean something special and *sound* like it means something special, then I don't do it. It makes me queasy. So, someone else does it for me. If I know I can't do it in a proper and better than average way, then why try? I think the right thing to do is to get someone who *can do it right* do it.

It won't hurt as much.

"What you really need is a government job," Dakota said. "Good pay. Good benefits. I've been thinking about this a lot. I'm going to get a government job."

"You don't speak French," I said.

"I'm Native," he said.

"You need French," I said.

"French trumps Native?" Dakota asked.

"Yeah," I said.

"Well, you got French, why don't you get a government job?"

"I'm English, asshole."

"So Native trumps English but not French."

"Yeah," I said. "You get French and you pretty much got your pick of jobs. The only person who would beat you would be a Native woman who speaks French and has a disability."

"We are a nation of polite idiots," Dakota said.

"That we are, my friend," I said. "That we are. Now write down who I am."

So Dakota wrote my speech. After I read it into the tape recorder thing and I realized I didn't really know what the hell I had just read, I decided maybe I should answer the rest of the questions myself, otherwise I'd sound like arty effeminate types who get their nails done but it's okay because it's metrosexual, and it's really not okay. A straight man should only get his nails done if he contracted some fungus or something and the doctor thought it would be a good idea to keep the nails manicured.

Liz seemed to tolerate Dakota in the beginning but now she seems awkward around him.

"You find Liz yet?"

"Nah."

My first weekend away from Liz, we had a big fight about a dog. She wanted a dog. I didn't want a dog. Sure, we have access to a backyard, but the apartment is too small and it costs too much and why? What are you going to do with a dog? They're big, they're messy and how do they get along with kids? But she was upset – she said she always wanted a dog. But then I had to leave and it was sort of awkward.

"I have to go now."

"I know."

"I'm not walking out, Wren, I have to go."

"I know."

No stupid dogs.

"There better not be a dog in my place when I get back."

I was out of town for the whole weekend. Liz was home without me for the whole weekend. My girlfriend was separated from me for a whole weekend. I probably should have called her but I didn't. I figured she was at the SPCA every day staring at the cute little mutts wagging their tails and looking up at you with big wide puppy eyes. I figured she'd go with Nina. I imagined her figuring out which little dog was apartment-sized and shorthaired. I figured she'd get some sort of terrier or terrier mix. I probably should have called. I never even picked up the phone once.

She could have called me.

The weekend passed.

Monday, the night I returned from my weekend, was hockey night with the guys. Liz wasn't home yet from work. The guys arrived my place about a half an hour before the game – Liz never came home from work – she must have gone out with Nina and the others right after her shift.

I thought she'd come home first but when suppertime came and passed without a sound, I realized she must have gone out. She's done that before; she just changes at work. It was no skin off my nose. It was just kind of weird since the last conversation we had was a fight and then we never saw each other all weekend.

"Where's the beer, man?" Dakota said. Dakota didn't go away for the weekend.

A dusty telephone.

Dakota doesn't much like the guys these days: Peter is *dense*, Bill is *petty* and *obsessive*, George is *not funny* and Harry is the *ultimate loser*.

Liz watches hockey.

Peter is a guy we knew from Dalhousie University in Halifax; Bill is a guy who worked at a bar with Dakota and me one summer at this resort in the Rockies; George is a friend of Bill's and George has a shitload of hockey equipment. Eventually we stopped calling Harry, poor guy drove everyone nuts, and that was pretty much when we started hanging out with my little brother Dave.

"Is this the room for beer-drinking cocksuckers?" Dave asked when he arrived. He thought it was funny. It wasn't.

"So, uh Eddy, you seen those big-screen TVs? When are you going to get a big-screen TV?" George said. George was quick to change an uncomfortable situation. "They're on sale at TVs Etc."

"Aren't big screens *fucking* awesome?" Peter said. He was drooling; you just knew it was his lifelong goal to own a big-screen TV. He could quote all recent prices: from department stores, to specialty stores to personal dealers, and give you run downs of the benefits and features of any given machine for sale in the local area. Maybe even in Seattle. Peter stood and started measuring the area where the big-screen TV would *someday* stand. He was drawing large squares with his hands, talking about cable and wiring problems.

"When do you think you'll get one?" Peter blurted.

"As soon as his girlfriend lets him," Dakota said.

I said nothing because, first, I was being egged on and, second, Dakota is supposedly my best friend. What else can you do? Especially when you think you know why he says these things. And you're just not ready to confront them.

"But Liz is a great girl," Dave said.

And when you look at Dave with anger and frustration because he just doesn't get it, you sincerely intend to explain reality to him. It's a joke and he just doesn't get it and you want so badly to tell him, it's a joke. But when you turn and you see him, you don't see a twenty-year-old man holding a bottle of home-made beer, you see a five-year-old boy holding his two front teeth in his hand because Brad knocked them out and you had to pick them out of the dirt. Back then, you told him people did things they didn't mean. And that's about the size of it.

"But Liz is good to Eddy."

The guys were in hysterics.

Ha. Ha. Ha. Ha. Ha.

Dave was genuinely confused; he couldn't detect the sarcasm and thought Dakota was insulting Liz. To an extent, Dakota was insulting Liz, but he was mainly saying it because he thought it sounded like a good joke. He made all the guys laugh and then everyone teased me for the longest three-and-a-half minutes in my entire life.

You could hate Dakota for putting you through an embarrassing three-and-a-half minutes or you could just let it pass. When it comes to things that are important, Dakota is there and that's what counts. At least, you think he's there for the important things.

"But Liz is great," Dave was still saying. He was grabbing my arm but I didn't want to talk about it; Liz wasn't home yet. "What's going on? I thought you and Liz were getting married."

"And Eddy is a *great* guy. Where's my *Mouseketeer* hat? Has anyone seen my *little mouseketeer* hat?" Dakota said. He glanced about the room with his best poker face while the guys laughed. Except Dave, of course. Dave had no idea what was going on. Clueless. Ma called it naive. Ma always said Dave was too nice to notice when people were being hurtful.

Dave wasn't much better than Harry, but he's my little brother; everyone knew his question was supposed to be a joke, and probably even Dakota made that same joke some other time. Coming from Dave it sounded weird, but we laughed anyway. Dave has a lot to learn about the art of joking. It didn't take a genius to feel the tension. That only made Dave sweat; maybe he doesn't know what a joke is but he sure knows what tension is. He laughed uneasily and stared at his hands.

Dave was eager to fit in.

When Dave was little – like maybe only five or six – he wanted me to like him so much that he trudged through a swamp to get my soccer ball. There was a bunch of neighbourhood kids playing around with the ball when it got kicked from the field and landed in the middle of this swamp. He got all excited about retrieving it for me. He hit a deep part and got stuck in the mud. I was maybe twelve. He started crying.

"Come on, baby."

"I'm coming."

He couldn't get loose and he started wailing. The ball sank into the mud. He lost both of his shoes and one sock. He did nothing right and that made him cry harder. I had to go in and get him.

"I lost the ball," he kept saying over and over again. He was crying so hard that there was mucus stuck to his face. The other kids were laughing at him.

I was all mad by the time I got to him. Mud everywhere. The ground was squishy. It stank like rotting garbage and sewage. You never knew when you were going to sink in the filth. All the kids were hollering. I was going to smack Dave when I reached him. My sneakers were trashed.

A little bird was tangled in some wires and twigs. It was greyish brown just like the twigs so it was hard to see. It had a broken wing. It was opening its mouth and squealing only there was no sound coming out. It was horrible. The beak was moving and moving and there was nothing happening. It looked like it was staring at me. With these solid black eyes that looked like holes.

Hollow eyes.

The bird needed help.

After I pulled Dave out of the mud and found the ball, I took the bird. I had to. I told the other kids Dave got stuck because he was trying to save the bird.

Dave smiled all proud.

The bird was in my care. Ma was all proud of me; she called all mothers in the neighbourhood and they talked about it. Da told me to be careful.

A damaged bird won't make it.

"Eddy's looking after a little bird with a broken wing. It's a wren."

Da helped me set up a box for it in the back porch. I let Dave help me. The sick wren became the *thing* in the neighbourhood. All the kids asked us about the bird and how it was doing.

One day when Dave and I went to check on the bird, its mouth wasn't squealing anymore. It was dead. Brad had crushed it in the palm of his hand.

"Don't let things suffer for your amusement."

Dave wailed. You never did.

Your brother takes a little more time than most people.

Dave's biggest problem is that he wants everyone else to like him so he tries *too* hard to fit in – the guys are hamming it up, saying rude things to each other (but you know it's all a joke) and so Dave tries to joke with us. But the real problem with Dave is that he wants so badly to fit in; his jokes aren't funny. *He does whatever it takes to fit in.* That's the real problem. So, sometimes, Dave can be rude, crude and downright vulgar. Dave is good with other things; like getting beer and helping out with furniture moves and all the little shit that goes on in your life. He is a generous kind of guy; he just doesn't always *get it.*

"What's so funny?" Dave asked. "I was a Mouseketeer. Some of those people are really famous now. Were you guys Mouseketeers? Remember, Eddy? You me and Brad."

No Brad.

"Where's the real beer?" George asked. He grimaced so hard that you could see his receding hairline. He was swirling a bottle of the homemade stuff and looking for sediment to settle on the bottom. We are good Grapes-R-Us patrons and there is no sediment at the bottom of our bottles, but it does have a strong aftertaste. I didn't blame George for not wanting to drink the homemade beer, but I thought it would have been nice if he had tried at least one. But George is the type of guy who can't even change types of salad dressing.

Dakota was laughing at him.

"Hey," George said. He was flustered. "Don't make me drink this fucking homemade shit."

"It'll put hair on your chest," Dakota told him.

"You like hair on a man's chest, do you, Dakota?" Dave asked. Again, with the unfunny jokes. It can be painful. "It's good, huh? I have hair on my chest."

"That's nice, Dave."

"You want to see?"

"What is this? A show and tell?" George asked. Good old George. He tossed a real beer to Dave and then one to Dakota. Peter and Bill were trying not to laugh; we all know that Dakota only has a sense of humour when he's the one doling out the humour. It was funny that Dave decided to idolize Dakota.

Only Dakota never saw it that way.

"Sit back down, there, pal."

"I can open your beer for you," Dave asked Dakota. Dakota smiled but it wasn't a true smile, rather, it was a dark sarcastic smile that ate the souls of small children. You could see it in his eyes.

"That's all right, Dave," Dakota said dryly. "Thanks anyway."

"Who has popcorn?" Bill asked. His hair is really curly and whenever he asks for popcorn, I imagine popcorn getting tangled in his hair and it kind of makes me laugh. But telling a guy you're thinking about his hair is just not something you do.

"I can't eat any butter on that. Penelope has me on a diet." Peter is always on a diet even though he could probably stand to gain five or ten pounds. Personally, I just think it's funny that his girlfriend's name is Penelope and his name

Susan Farrell

is Peter. He calls her Penny so they're Peter and Penny. It would be funny if they named their kids Perry and Patty.

"Just put the fucking game on already." Peter has no patience.

"The game doesn't start for another fifteen minutes, big boy," I said.

"Then there's time for popcorn," Bill said again. "All right! Dry air-popped popcorn, here we come!"

And like the great host that I am, I went to put some popcorn on: one bowl with buttered popcorn and one bowl with *freaking* non-buttered popcorn for those of us on diets. Liz has never said anything to me, but I watch the fat anyway. She could get any guy she wanted. She can tell me time and time again that she doesn't care what the man looks like but when she fantasizes about a lover, I'm willing to bet, he doesn't have an extra chin. You don't see too many movie leads with potbellies and love handles.

The kitchen door opened behind me.

"Is your brother a fag or what?" Dakota muttered. His face was tight and his teeth were clenched; he was bent out of shape over something. He followed me into the kitchen like we were women going to the bathroom. If you only had a lipstick, then you could commemorate the event.

"What?"

"Your brother, man, your little brother. Huh?"

"Hey Dakota, relax. Have a beer."

"You'd tell me if he was, right?"

"Yeah."

"Dave tells all these. What would you call them? Jokes? And they're just a little *off*, and he looks at you a little too long like a woman would. He sits a little too close and he patted my butt," Dakota had to stop ranting because I was laughing at him.

You don't want to laugh at someone when they're having a *tender* moment because everyone has their sore spots and the last thing you want to do is poke someone's sore spot but sometimes, well, sometimes, the sore spot is just too silly. But when you laugh at a sore spot, you get a defensive reaction. Dakota got nervous; you could see it in his eyes. "What? Is he? So he is? What? What the *fuck* is so funny, you ugly white boy?"

"Well, I don't *know* if he's gay. How the fuck am I going to know something like that? That's *personal*. That's Dave's business and his girlfriend's business. I'm laughing cause you think he'd be *interested in you*. That's funny. You think the whole world is in love with you, don't you?"

"The whole world is," Dakota said.

Two lonely nights. Three lonely days.

Sometimes you find your friends witty and sarcastic and that's a good thing. But just sometimes when you hear the words they're saying and you see the cocky little smile on their wretched little *autumn sunshine* face, you can't help but think they're a career asshole and then you wonder why women ever fall for such career assholes. And you wonder, have you ever used such shit on a woman? And you wonder how long it's going to be before Liz slaps your face and tells you to move on. And what is going through her weird little mind that she'd fall for such stupid shit? How can she possibly take in this garbage?

"You can be such a pompous shit."

"Excuse me?"

"Come one now, sometimes, you can have a pretty big ego. Give us all a break."

"What the fuck is eating you?" Dakota said.

There are times when you should say *something*. You need to know certain things and the only way you're ever going to find out is to ask. There's only one way to find out.

You have to ask. You're not going to know the answer if you don't ask the question. But by the same token, that's also the same way you can keep the peace. You don't ask - you don't ever have to know. When you think about it, why do you have to know everything? There are times when you shouldn't say anything.

"Just don't pick on my little brother, man. He just wants you to like him. He's joking – the same way you are. You come into my place, you have respect."

"I have respect. You know I have respect."

"Then lay off Dave, you know what he's like."

Pressing against the counter, Dakota leaned back and sighed. He didn't believe a word I had just said – he knew I wasn't concerned about my brother. Dakota's not an idiot; he knew something else was bothering me but he also knows me well enough not to bother me. I opened a beer.

"How was the weekend?" I asked. "You see Liz at all?"

"Just give me a beer."

I met Dakota when he was getting the shit kicked out of him.

When Dakota was twelve, his alcoholic father dropped dead in their family kitchen. Heart attack. Totally unexpected. He had never had a heart condition prior to this incident and there had been no warning at all: no health problems, no abnormal behaviour other than the violent drinking, no new allergies, nothing. Dakota was the only kid home; he has three brothers, but they're all older than him and they had all moved out by the time this happened. His mother wanted him to stay home from school that day but Dakota didn't listen to her.

Dakota never really liked his father – a lot of violence, a lack of love, an absence of understanding. Maybe if his brothers were in the family home when he was growing up, things would have been different. But Dakota wasn't exactly a planned child and his brothers were long gone. His mother never intervened because mothers don't intervene. Dakota knows that, but he never went to her funeral and now his three brothers, who already called him *apple Indian*, won't talk to him. So, when things are bad, Dakota likes to pretend things are normal. That means – stick with the routine.

Dakota went to school the day his father died.

He missed his first class because he had to help the ambulance drivers and he had to calm his mother. When he got to school, someone commented on the redness in his eyes, which led to the redness in his skin, which led to one angry Dakota, which led to what the media and Halifax *Chronicle Herald* reported as – *Three white boys attack Native American boy in local high school.* It all took place in the back parking lot beneath the elm trees.

That's where I come in.

That's when I met Dakota.

You'd like to say you thought it was noble or ethical or some other great deed of humanity or something like that. Anything that gives you an ounce of greatness, but that's just not the case. There was no thought in your head at all; your head was empty. You were standing in the parking lot waiting for your little sister to get her things together so you could walk her home. You saw the brawl; you saw three guys on one guy and so you jumped in. There was no ingenious thought. No premeditation at all. It was all gut reaction.

Fights should be fair.
Three guys on one guy isn't fair.
This fight isn't fair.

My nose got broken that day and Dakota got a scar on his collarbone, but we pummelled two of those guys real good. One of them started wailing like a little girl. The third guy was too big. You thought for sure he was going to snap your arm off like a piece of cookie when suddenly, the school door opens and your baby sister walks out. Other times, you hated it when she screams and cries but not on that day. She saw the blood on your face.

"Eddy! Eddy! Don't you hurt my brother! You animal!"

Teachers came running. The third guy took off. You sat on the curb and rubbed your arm and shoulder to make sure all the necessary parts were still intact. Dakota just lay on the ground breathing heavy. We were both covered in blood. But the teachers gathered around my little sister because she was crying so hard.

Dakota and I laughed. We were friends after that.

We laminated the article that appeared in the Halifax *Chronicle Herald.*

I met his family only once before his mother died: his mother, two aunts and two sisters. Dakota couldn't wait to get away. He talked about it. Every day. Every day was the same fucking story – *university will get me out of here.*

"You boys drink a lot of beer," his mother said. "Too much beer. Your father drank too much beer. Your brothers drink too much beer."

His mother had that same evil scary look in her eyes that my mother did. She wanted Dakota to get an education.

You do what you're told.

University is the golden dream.

We were all sitting on the front stoop drinking beers; it was someone's birthday. She slapped me in the face for saying "fuck" in front of her. Then she held my face in her hands.

"He drinks to sedate himself," his mother told me. "So do you."

"I'm sorry," I said.

She pointed her finger at me.

Dakota's mother was a poet too. Maybe it was genetic. We were only in high school.

That's all I remember about Dakota's family. I think they're all dead now. They seemed to be dying. He's the only guy I know who has a box of funeral cards and sympathy cards.

"See you later, Eddy," Dave said.

Hockey night was over. Hockey night was over and Dakota had slipped out early. Hockey night was over and Liz still wasn't home.

I never make love to Liz after the guys have been over. Hockey all night. Too much beer. Too much popcorn. Too much cursing. Too much of everything that does not put me in the mood. I was in the mood for Liz, but I wasn't in the mood for sex.

Sitting on the bed, I did some crosswords until I heard the key in the lock. As she entered the bedroom, dressed in a short white dress, she dropped her purse on the floor and straddled me. She was wearing a short white dress but it had a matching jacket. Her legs were long and slender; she looked silky from head to toe. The curve in her thigh slid into the curve in her calf and then the curve in her ankle fit perfectly into her shoes – she was streamlined. She had a white scarf in her hair. She yanked the scarf out, her hair fell loose in wild curls, and she wrapped the scarf around my neck.

"Hey tiger," she said. Her eyes were bright and glossy and she kissed my chin. Her hair tickled my neck. She smelled like ice cream. "Hmmm, stubble."

"Want to watch some TV?" I asked.

She giggled. She ran her fingers through my hair and then kissed me.

"How was the weekend?" I asked.

We held hands.

"Uneventful," she said.

She kissed me again. Sliding her down off of me, I snuggled her into my body. Dejected, she stopped caressing me and we were still for a while.

"Everything all right?" she asked

"Dakota was an ass tonight."

"Oh," she said.

Again, we were quiet.

Say you hate him.

"Well," she muttered. "I'm sorry to hear that. Did he spoil the hockey game for you and the others?"

"No, no. But he was picking on Dave."

"Hmmm, Dave's sweet and all, but he is an easy target. He thinks the word 'masturbate' refers to a university degree. I'm sure it was just Dakota's weird sense of humour."

Tell me you hate him.

"Oh, yeah, you're probably right. He was getting on my nerves. Does Dakota ever get on your nerves?"

Tell me you can't stand to be around him.

"Uh, huh. How were the rest of the guys?" She kissed me again and rested her head on my shoulder.

Say it.

"Fine. They were all fine."

You're not saying it.

The guys were the same: same jokes, same beer. Dave was relatively new to the gang and he wanted everyone to take up scuba diving. That's new. I doubt that anyone will go for it though. Harry was a good guy though; you don't get rid of a guy because he gets married. What kind of a plan is that? Dakota is scared because he doesn't know what he wants. That is the fear you cannot purge.

"We had a good time," Liz said. "A lot of dancing."

"Was Colette there?"

"I don't really see her anymore."

She snuggled into me and gave me a squeeze. She sighed and it sounded like it might have been a mushy moment but then she just smiled and kissed me on the cheek. She buried her face into my neck.

"Oh, Eddy," she whispered.

Oh, Eddy.

Nothing followed.

I cheated on my girlfriend, told her about it, got into a fight with her about something she's wanted her whole life and then I left her alone for the weekend with my best friend who happens to be a man-whore.

Liz:

Human Feces was the title of an artistic piece at the Art Gallery. It was actual human feces and stranger still, someone bought it.

"Where you display the human feces in your house, hmm?" this blonde woman said to me.

She elbowed me and we both giggled. We weren't really laughing at the exhibit so much as we were laughing at the fact that someone had paid a great deal of money to own it. Where do you display "human feces"?

Her name was Colette. She was born in Paris, lived in Switzerland, Germany and Japan, attended university in the United States and then moved to Canada. She liked Vancouver so much that she stayed. She said she enjoyed the purple quality of the Coastal Mountains.

Colette had short blonde hair cut in a bob and she had braces when I met her; this was a gift from her father. Colette was into reconstructive surgery: she had had her nose done the year before and her chin broken and re-set over the holidays. Her breasts were augmented, nipples centred, her thighs had been sucked, her eyebrows had been pumped and she wasn't a natural blonde, of course. Even her eyes were a fake jade green. She was younger than me and she complained about being old.

Colette was my fancy European friend.

After that moment, we enrolled in art classes together – the human body, water painting, ink drawing, ceramics.

"I had a dream, which was not all a dream." Lord Byron.

She looked perfect and men looked at her like she was perfect but none of it was real. That didn't seem to matter.

"It gives me the feeling of power," she explained to me. "And a lot of people think green is a colour of money and power. It is like the aphrodisiac."

Every Monday and Wednesday evening, we took some sort of art class at one of the colleges or community centres and there was usually a downtown adventure afterwards: an art gallery, a theatre, a club, a pool hall, or perhaps the latest greasy spoon diner. Colette knew all the trendy places. Mostly, she knew what was passé, and we would never go there, of course. In downtown, the trendy and the passé change every other week so it's difficult to keep track but Colette always knew. She would laugh at herself because she always *knew*.

"Stick with me, baby."

Women help women.

Eddy liked her.

"You can do female things with her," he said.

"What's that? Talk about menstruation and sex?"

"Nah, *sex* is *man* talk."

"Eddy!"

Eddy said anything for a laugh.

After a final glaze and all the finishing touches were done, our ceramic Elvis heads, (mine was white and Colette had dyed hers a deep forest green) were complete. Plopping them in the back seat of Colette's bright green convertible, we drove to my place. The finished heads were fairly large and heavy and the hair was flat and smooth: a glass would rest comfortably on top.

We showed Eddy the Elvis heads. He laughed. He didn't just laugh – he guffawed.

"Wren," he said with a gleam in his eyes. He patted the Elvis head and smiled. "Who are we *giving* it to?"

"Eddy!"

He kissed me on the cheek, cracked open a cola and trudged into the living room. We could still hear him chuckling and that made us chuckle. We made cucumber and cream cheese sandwiches and sat outside beneath the elm trees. It was one of the first days of the spring season and it wasn't raining.

"Your boyfriend is a real catch," Colette said. She winked.

Eddy was a real catch.

On a Sunday afternoon, we found ourselves downtown at some cute cafe – there were pictures of spotted cows and brightly dressed gnomes everywhere – a place that would make Eddy feel ill. Salads were more expensive than main entrees. But the waiter was cute and everyone in the place had thick French accents. Besides, Colette was actively single and whenever she espied men, we had to be there.

"What do you think I'd look like with red hair?" she asked.

"You're not going to change again, are you?"

"Change is how we adapt. If you can't change, then you can't adapt. What do you say we get tattoos this weekend?"

What are you adapting to?

"I don't know about that."

"Oh, I'm sorry. Do you have to check with *the man* first?"

Even at the moment she asked, the question irked me. Her eyes flinched a little and then she looked away. Her hand tightened around the fork and she jabbed a chunk of cheddar. Suddenly, the waiter became far more interesting than the conversation. Colette was an avid talker.

Fast-forward. Rewind. Play. Record.

"And then I thought we could paint in the park. Lots of people do. If the sun is out, it could lots of fun. We could bring your boyfriend. He could be our model. He could pose for us – bare-chested, of course," she said. "Nudes are great."

She sighed dreamily and her gaze drifted off into the distance. When she realized I was watching her, she laughed. She squeezed my hand.

"It's a joke, silly," she said. She twirled her hair around her finger. "A joke! God! Do you take everything so seriously? Here, let's get the waiter with the ponytail to take our picture. He is such a handsome man."

Eddy didn't care for the picture.

Nina didn't care for the picture either. The picture was simple: Colette, the French waiter and me. He had his arms around both of us – he had the biggest smile. Nina said that

I looked unhappy and my curly hair reminded her of the seventies. Anything from the seventies scared Nina. She thought I looked too much like ABBA although she wasn't quite sure which woman. But Nina loathed Colette from the first time she laid eyes on her.

People don't do such things.

Colette strutted into Lucy's in the middle of a rainstorm. She let out a decidedly feminine shriek once inside and shook herself like a wet cat. She was wearing a red plastic raincoat, a red plastic beret, red pumps and she was carrying a bright red umbrella. A man had stopped to open the door for her. He left, but only after he knew she was *safely* inside the store. Safe from *what*, none of us were really certain, but Colette thought the man was an *absolute doll*. She gushed about him for quite some time after he had gone.

"He's a bald man in a suit! He must be rich!" she said with a wink. It was a joke but the others didn't find it amusing. Humour has a tendency to be familial.

Noriko laughed nervously. She glanced at me and offered a weak smile then began pricing the new earrings, bracelets and necklaces. It was more than I expected. Colette strolled around the shop.

"So what did you do with your Elvis head?" Nina asked her.

"I gave it to Daddy," she said as she fingered through our assortment of silk scarves. "He just thinks the world of all the dead Hollywood types."

"That sure is a great deal of people," Nina said. Her voice was flat.

As Colette entered the jewellery section, Noriko darted into the hat section casting furtive glances but saying nothing as usual. She avoided direct eye contact with me so I assumed that meant she didn't want an introduction.

Ginger absorbed a good long look and then made herself scarce. Eventually, Nina ended conversation attempts and made like there was pressing business to attend to at the cash register. And Colette followed her, attempting another conversation so Nina excused herself from us and slipped into the back room.

Colette turned to me and shrugged her shoulders. She dried her nose with a tissue and powdered her face with perfumed talc. She dragged me to the mirror in the sunglasses section and brushed my hair.

"Some women are jealous of other women," Colette said matter-of-factly. "You must know what I mean – you probably have had this problem, hmmm?"

While I thought about my answer, I noticed that Noriko was watching us. Her face was wan and her brow was scrunched up into little knots. She busied herself with the price gun when she realized she had been caught – she saw me looking at her via the mirror.

"Do you want your hair up or down?" Colette asked. She was holding the bulk of my hair in her hand.

"Down," I said.

"You look like the mystery with your hair down, eh?"

"I'm more comfortable," I told her.

"But you look like the elegant with the hair up. You like, no?"

Ginger and Nina were laughing in the back room; their hushed giggles sent a chill up and down my spine. Colette was brushing my hair again. Her face had lost her perky smile. Her eyes grew distant and she sighed. The brush strokes were slow and methodical. She seemed pensive.

"I think you and I should go to Hawaii. Have you ever been? Would your man let you go with me or does he not trust me, eh?"

I don't know. *Je ne sais pas.*

Before we left Lucy's, Colette had bought a few hundred dollars worth of items: an antique choker and matching earrings, a couple of silk scarves, a fake fur jacket and knee-high boots. She squealed and squeezed my hand as each item was rung in. She had them all wrapped in tissues and decorative boxes – Noriko prepared all the items in the back room. Colette used her father's credit card for the purchase.

Nina said nothing. She merely took the card, ran it through the machine, and awaited approval like she does with every other credit card user. The left side of her mouth was twitching uncontrollably and her neck muscles were tight. But she was quiet and the gracious customer service smile never left her face once. The etiquette man would have been proud.

Visa or MasterCard?

Nina and the others were supposed to have lunch with us but that didn't happen. After Nina said she couldn't make it (due to some unforeseen and immediate business concern), Ginger remembered she had to have lunch with her husband (he was anxious to see her) and Noriko remembered a test (it was a last minute quiz) she had to study for or her 3.97 GPA would suffer. So, Colette and I skipped lunch, grabbed dark roast coffee and sesame bagels, and hung out at the Big Men Gym instead.

If Colette had felt awkward, she never let on.

We were sitting in one of our favourite lunch spots, Rainy Day Coffee Shop, after an afternoon walk through the flower gardens at Queen Elizabeth Park. The sun was shining. The sky was peacock blue. There were face painters, musicians, artists painting portraits for ten dollars and buskers of all kinds. It was June and tourist season was alive and kicking. The air smelled like lilacs and there were cocker spaniels and babies everywhere. After some flirtatious smiles and sweet giggles, Colette managed to get our favourite table by the indoor fountain. Life was good. Coffee refills were free. Eddy had gone to refill our mugs.

"How is the eggplant?" she asked me.

"Not bad," I said. (I don't remember the taste.) "But they must have a new chef. This sauce is just not as good as it used to be."

"Such is the stuff of life, yes?"

Eddy knocked over one of the metal cream containers; a waiter had to assist him. The two laughed with each other as they wiped up the mess on the condiment stand. From the way Eddy was motioning his hands and arms, they were talking about sports, particularly hockey. His fingers were moving in quick succession denoting fast moves and scores by his favourite players.

"What's he like in bed?" Colette whispered. Her voice was hushed and breathy; she spoke stiffly, without moving her lips. She watched Eddy and the waiter at the condiment stand as she spoke. Smiling at me, there was a gleam in her fake green eyes as she bit into a radish.

"I like him," I stated coldly.

"Hmmm, *like*, eh? I want details! Spill, little girl. How does he kiss?"

Eddy waved over at us. Holding two mugs for us to see, he placed them on the counter. He held up the sugar containers and the milk. We directed, in a very awkward manner, which condiments we wanted. Colette was giggling like a Catholic schoolgirl who had never seen a boy before. She kept saying how sweet and charming he was. She kept calling Eddy a *pet*.

"Well, Colette," I said. I hesitated. "That's sort of a personal question."

"If he is ever my boyfriend, I would know anyway. Then we could compare notes, eh!"

The statement took awhile to digest. Sometimes, when people say things, they don't realize the implications. They're talking to make conversation or to say daring things because they think it's cute and entertaining or what-have-you. If that's the case, then one shouldn't overreact. One should just accept the inappropriate statement as is and move on. Why make an issue out of a non-issue? But all the same, there was a pang in my chest that seemed to echo in my throat. Tightness. Asphyxiation.

Eddy placed the mugs in front of us. His knuckles were flushed from the animated hockey anecdotes. He was wearing his favourite brown woollen sweater. He was still talking about hockey when he approached us.

Just hold me.

My Eddy. My sweetheart. My lover. My best friend. The man who bleached my red shirt and turned all of our clothes pink. It wasn't funny then and to think of it, it's still not funny. He blushes with anger whenever he thinks about it. But they are just clothes.

"Ah," Colette said. "You take such good care of us, Eddy. You certainly know how to treat a woman."

Eddy blushed.

"Hey, Wren, I, uh, saw Peter and Penny over by the window so I'm just going to say hello."

Kissing the top of my head, he brushed his hand over Colette's hair as he walked away. She smiled and touched his hand as he passed. He looked back at me, slightly confused. When he sat down with Peter and Penny, he put his back to us. Moments later, Penny stole curious glances at Colette.

"That's one of Eddy's friends," I explained.

"She's not very pretty," Colette said.

Colette was stirring her coffee with her finger. She licked the black liquid off and sighed. She stared out the window at the trees and flowers and the city perched in the purple mountains.

"Oh," she said suddenly. She squeezed my hand. "I am so smitten with your boyfriend. It is too bad that we are friends. You won't hate me, will you?"

It was a statement that I didn't really hear – it sounded distant and far removed, like perhaps it was a voice on a television in some other room. The volume was too loud so I overheard. But as I glanced at Colette and saw her quiet frigid face staring back at me, I knew the statement was real. She was waiting for my response but I was still stunned.

"I don't think I understand you."

"I want your boyfriend."

"What are you talking about?"

"Anything's fair in love and war," she said. She stirred my coffee. "And I fully expect us to still be friends if I take your boyfriend away from you.... You're the first best friend I've had in a very long time, Liz. And I'd still be friends with you if you took my boyfriend."

Perhaps that is true. Perhaps that is the reality of other people, many other people. Knowing Colette, it probably is. But regardless of whether or not it's true, it's irrelevant because that's just not how I see myself.

Myself.

"That's Colette on the phone again," Eddy said.

Seventeen down – lessening. I motioned that I was not here.

"She's not here," Eddy said.

Eddy was confused (pretending to be is more like it) but only momentarily. He quickly returned to the phone and told her I had already left with some other friends. I heard him laugh repeatedly while on the phone and I could imagine all the cute little jokes and witty sayings she was telling him. I wondered how much longer she would keep calling; it had already been over a week and I hadn't accepted any of her eighteen calls. I wondered if she would just start asking Eddy to meet her places. I wondered if he'd go.

Hold me.

"So, uh, you're not taking calls from Colette anymore?"

"I'm tired, Eddy."

Please hold me.

The smiling lines faded from around his eyes and his mouth and as he sat beside me and stared into my eyes, I felt that he *knew*. He clicked the TV off and breathed heavily. For a moment, we just sat very still. Together. The old sofa seemed much larger than when we first bought it years ago, the square cushions were fluffier, and we sank down in the pillows. We were quiet.

Somewhere outside the basement suite, a dog was barking.

Eddy put his arms around me and totally enveloped me. His heart was beating in my eardrums and when I shut my eyes, everything felt wonderful. When he holds me like that, I feel like I am sixteen all over again and discovering the world for the first time. Anything is possible and everything is a possibility. His arms feel like a sacred haven. I feel safe.

Eddy could always make me feel safe.

5. Current situation.

In your estimation, what has been the most important or significant conversation in which you have participated?

Eddy:

"Eddy, you are a man of *immediate* wants."

"What the *fuck* does that mean?"

"It means that you are a man of immediate wants."

"Yeah? Well, Dakota, you are a rat *ass* bug-fucker."

"*What* does that mean?"

"It means you are a rat ass bug-fucker."

"Eddy, Eddy, *Eddy*, what are we going to do with you?"

"Well, think of this, anus breath, how the hell am I ever going to understand you if you don't fucking explain things? Huh, flesh-head? Or can't you *explain* things, there, Mr. Big University?"

Anus breath.

"Oh, I can explain things just fine. It's just that *stupid* white boys like yourself can't understand."

"Hey, Dakota, man, that was freaking racist. I thought *university* people weren't freaking racist."

"I can't be racist. I'm not *white*."

"Ain't that a sweet smelling shit! Okay, Mr. University Fuck-Wise, what does this freaking 'racist' mean, then, huh? *Ex-plain* to me – racist."

"Oh, that's such a big-ass question for such a little man. Just answer this, are you or are you not a stupid white boy?"

"I am a stupid white boy."

"There you have it. Now it's not racist."

"Why isn't it racist?"

"How *can it* be racist? Where's your fucking head? You're fucking *white*. It can't be racist when you're white."

The words in your head.

"What do you mean?"

Go round and round.

"Eddy, man, how can it be racist? You're white and you're saying you're *white*. It's okay to say whatever you want about your own self and that's just, shit! I don't know what that is!"

Round and round.

"So I'm allowed to say I'm white, but I'm not allowed to say you're – what double-fucking colour are you anyway?"

"I see myself as autumn sunshine."

Magenta.

"Autumn sunshine. *Sweet*. So listen, *sunshine*, am I supposed to *pretend* I don't notice we're different colours? If I can notice that I'm white then I must notice you're *sweet sunshine*."

"That's autumn to you, pal. Autumn sunshine. Well. You *notice* but you can't say anything. Look, it doesn't matter. To call yourself a stupid white boy is not racist. What the fuck do you care anyway, man? I thought you wanted to sound educated."

"Hey, watch it, you Indian shithead."

Words go round and round. Round and Round.

"That's racist, you pig-fucker."

"Dakota, man, taste me and the horse I rode in on."

Susan Farrell

"I'm telling you, little *monsieur sucker de cock*, that's racist and I'm frigging offended."

"You're my *friend*, Mr. Ratshit. You know I'm not racist. Why the hell are you saying it's *racist*?"

"Okay, Eddy, because I'm your friend and I love you, I'll simplify the reality of the situation for you. Here's your *simple* rule: you're *white*, asshole. Every *fucking* thing you say is racist. That's your sweeping generalization. Got that? Ready? Repeat after me. I am white. I am a white straight male. I am twenty-eight-years old."

"Oh, hey wait, is this the speech for number one you're writing for me? Are you going to make me look like I'm short a gonad or what's the story? Can I trust you or are you fucking with me? I want to look reasonably *good*, you know. I'm with Liz, remember? I got to be good."

The interior made her cry.

"What's this 'for Liz' business? You don't appreciate a woman like Liz. You're with Liz because of her tits. She's a sweet honeyfuck. You don't even *like* Liz."

Can I just think about it? That's a big decision.

"I love Liz."

"Whatever gets you through the night."

"I love Liz."

Liz. Liz. Liz.

"Where's Liz anyway?"

"I don't know."

I think we should have children.

"I thought the whole freaking point of this psychology tape was that you do it together."

"Nah, Dakota. You don't understand how relationships work. You don't read the rules too good. You know if you only read *between the lines*, then you're never going to know what's *actually* happening in the real world. We have to do it at the same time. Not *together*. There's a difference, eh?"

"Whatever. Just hurry up and piss and get out of the loo, buddy. I got to take a leak."

"You can piss out back beneath the elm trees. I'll piss when I'm damn good and ready."

The urine in your dick.

"So where is Liz?"

Goes round and round.

"I don't know. I thought she was around here somewhere."

Liz:

Young people today are going nowhere without an education.

Bankruptcy.

"Um, uh, hi, I'm not really sure if I called the right place. I'm not really sure who I'm supposed to talk to actually. I don't know who. Uh, I'm calling about money problems. I need some financial help."

No one will help me.

"That's us. Department of Consumer Affairs. My name's Keiko, why don't you tell me your problem and I'll see if I can hook you up with one of our operators who specialize in that particular area. Okay? What's your name?"

"Liz."

"Okay, Liz, so what *seems* to be the problem?"

"Okay, thanks. Thanks. Uh, my student loan is way out of control and there's no money. I just, I just don't know what to do."

"Mmm, hmm, another student loan. Okay, let me just see if I can get you through to Kyszychda. Can you hold?"

88,840 dollars, they think. Plus interest.

"Can you hold?

"Okay."

Music.

No one will help me.

"Hello, Kyszychda speaking. How can I help?"

"Uh, hi, I'm having a problem with my student loan."

Bankruptcy.

"Hmmm, I see. Is that your only debt?"

"Yes."

"That *means* you have no other credit problems."

"No."

"*No* credit problems? That means you're *up to date* with your credit card payments?"

"Uh, I have no credit cards. I'm in debt. I'm in debt. I figured. Why should I get a credit card?"

"Right, right. So, it's just the student loan? Have you *graduated*?"

"Yes."

"Hmmm, then I recommend you get a job and pay off your student loan."

"Uh, see, that's my problem."

"Hmmm, so how much money are we talking about?"

"Around eighty-eight thousand, there seems to be some discrepancy with the amount."

"Hmmm, that's worrisome."

"Um, I know. So what do I do?"

"Who has your loan?"

"Um, I thought you guys had my loan. That's why I called."

"Where do you live? Are you in this city?"

"Yes, I live here now. There's no work in my town."

"Yeah. You're coming out here to take our jobs, yeah, I know. Of course. So what exactly sort of problem is it we're talking about here?"

"Exactly? Uh, I can't *pay it*. I need some sort of help to lower payments or something. I, uh, actually, I think I'm going to have to declare bankruptcy."

Bankruptcy.

"Student loans are not permitted to default. Hmmm, where is your loan?"

"I don't know what that means. What are you asking?"

88,840 dollars.

"I need to know where your loan is located."

"Uh. I gave you the number of the loan. The telephone number I called, this one, is on all of my documents. I called for assistance."

"What type of loan is this?"

"What's that? It's a student loan. Is that what you mean?"

"Hmmm, you can only claim bankruptcy for your personal debt issues, excluding your student loan. What is your personal debt load?"

"My only debt is the student loan and it is personal."

"Student loans are not applicable. What do you mean you don't have any personal debts?"

No one will help me.

"I don't have any personal debts other than the student loan."

"Hmmm, I think it's too early for you to declare bankruptcy. Why don't you ask your parents to make the payments for a while? They like it when you pay the payments for a while. You should only have to pay about two hundred a month."

"Uh, actually my minimum payment is five hundred and eleven dollars a month. That's more than half my monthly income."

88,840 dollars.

Bankruptcy.

No one will help me.

"Lower the payments."

"Um, then, I need some help."

"You can lower your student loan payments through your bank representative at the proper branch."

"Um, banks don't lower payments. They told me to call you."

"True. True. Why can't you just pay what you can for the time being?"

"I just told you I don't have the money to make that size payment."

"Then have the bank lower your payment."

"But, uh, banks don't lower payments."

"Right, right."

"Um ... um, so what do I do?"

"You have to talk to you bank. They'll have a *special* representative – about lowering your student loan payments."

"Um, yes, I already talked to the bank personnel. Everyone in the bank, really and um. They told me to call *here*. Banks, uh, banks don't lower payments."

"Yes, I know banks don't lower payments. Do you work at all? Do you have a job?"

88,840 dollars.

"Yes, I work in retail. Lucy's Vintage Accessories. It's about thirty-four cents higher than minimum wage."

The interest is growing now.

"Yes, I suppose that is a bit of a problem."

"Yes, uh, I know, that – that is my problem, see? I physically can't. I don't have the money."

"Well, let's see, how long have you had this problem? Have you *given* yourself the required amount of interim time to get a job in your field? What was your degree in?"

"Philosophy."

The Bankrupt.

"Philosophy? Is that a real subject? What is that? The meaning of life? So you're probably going to have to claim bankruptcy."

"Um, okay, so how do I go about doing that?'

"Well, you can't just do that. And *we* don't do bankruptcy. Student loans are not applicable."

"Um.... what do you do?"

The Official Receiver.

"We just assist."

"Okay.... What am I supposed to do?"

"You'll have to lower the payments."

"Um, how do I do that?"

No one will help me.

"Talk to your bank."

6. Your sexual life.

To what degree are you satisfied or dissatisfied with your sexual relations with your partner? Do you discuss your attitudes and feelings regarding your sexual life with your partner?

Eddy:

Liz has great tits.

Liz has got curves everywhere and she kind of slinks when she walks and pouts her lips. You get hard when you watch her walk. Especially when she wears her heels and her little skirts. Her hair is long and dark with big curls and it flows past her shoulders and smells like strawberries and vanilla. Liz has big, blue eyes and she wears that eye makeup which gives her a seductive look. She wears a lot of low-cut shirts and she shows just a little bit of cleavage – not so much that you're staring at her all the time but enough that you notice.

Tits.

I notice Liz all the time.

Sometimes I think she sees me looking. She likes it. Her face will redden just a touch and she'll have to look the other way. She's so cute when she plays innocent. When I drop in her workplace unexpected, I can always turn her on. She smells like her expensive perfume, Scent de Europe, when she's at work. I'll just browse the hat and underwear wall.

Catch her eye every now and then and gaze at her a little too long.

I visited her at work.

"Can I help you with something, sir?" she asked.

She was using her customer service voice. She was standing directly behind me and she leaned in close so close that I could smell her *history* perfume and feel her breath against my neck. She ran her hand up my spine.

"I think I want these," I said calmly. I was acting like a customer. It was a pair of boxer shorts with a tartan. "Do they come in other colours?"

That was all I said.

Liz took my hand; her fingers traced little circles on my flesh. She shoved the curtain of the dressing room aside. Smiling graciously and somewhat artificially like a plastic sales clerk, she motioned me to go inside the booth. She was very formal.

"Why don't you try them on, sir?"

Who the hell tries on boxer shorts?

When I went in, she followed me. Before you could even figure out what was going on, she had her hand down your pants and her tongue in your mouth. She wasn't wearing any panties. It was the best ten minutes of my life.

After something like that, you make it a point to visit your girlfriend at work a little more often.

Big blue eyes.

Liz hasn't been smiling since we got back from the interior. She walks around with a dazed look on her face and she asks about when we're going to do the relationship study survey. She says *smiles are not to be taken for granted.* Liz might be a little too smart for her own good. She thinks *too much.*

Sometimes I just don't know what the fuck she's talking about. I mean I hear the words and I know they're English, hell, I even know it's a statement and there's a thought in there somewhere. But fuck if I can find it.

"I'm just trying to determine the reasonable degree of verisimilitude in Dakota's tentative working concept of what constitutes a friendship."

"Yeah?"

I'm just trying to determine the blah blah blah peanut butter up my ass take it outside who wants candy blah blah friendship.

Yeah.

"Dakota's not here, Wren."

"I'm worried about friendship," she said. It was like she wasn't talking to me; she was staring off into space. "I'm worried about your friendships."

"Dakota won't be around as much."

I'm just trying to determine the blah blah blah peanut butter up my ass take it outside what the fuck is that shit blah blah friendship.

When your girlfriend says something like that, you know it's time for a beer. You figure it might even be time to go out for a beer with the guys. You only wonder who can get away from their home and their girlfriend in such short notice. Peter always has something to do and his dog has been sick lately. George has been putting extra hours in at the shop so they can make a down payment. There's always a pub in the area, that's why they're called *neighbourhood houses.*

When you come home, she'll be all thought out. And you know what that means.

Sex.

Liz wears lingerie of all sorts. She has a thing for short silk dresses with sheer bustiers and thin dainty straps so her shoulders are bare. She likes them so they're a little too tight on her breasts and then the rest of the dress just hangs from her body and skirts across the top of her thighs. Sometimes, one of the straps will slide down her arm. That makes the bust part even tighter. I buy them for her at Dare You Boutique at the mall. She lets her hair loose and it falls down her back in big wavy curls. She dabs perfume behind her ears and she uses her finger to trace some down her neck and between her breasts. She puts on some specially mixed music she likes and dances just for me.

Sometimes she doesn't want me to touch her. She wants to dance and frolic to the music. She just likes to tease me, she just wants to know if she can get me hard. The answer is yes.

The strap is sliding off the round of her shoulder. Her breasts are tight in the bustier. Her nipples are hard and visible through the sheer silk. Her face is a little flushed with colour. She's wet. She's swaying slightly to the music. The silk dress is caressing her legs. She lets her hands glide across her whole body, just slightly touching herself. She pulls the other strap off her shoulder. She stays on the opposite side of the room so I can't touch her.

She thinks I don't know this but I do – I just pretend that I don't know. And other times, I think she's just fascinated with my dick.

She always wants to know how I like it.

"How do you like it?"

Good.

"Good."

"You hot?"

Ready to go.

"Yeah."

"Good and hard?"

Oh yeah.

"Yeah."

"Let me see."

"Yeah."

"Take your pants off."

"Yeah."

"You want me?"

"Yeah."

"Then fuck me."

Sex.

Liz is one hell of a woman. Liz can look hot in sheer black lace or baggy sweat pants. It's all in her attitude. She has a great walk. The look *is in her eyes.* I never really know what the hell she's going to say. Liz always makes me smile. You see her and it's instinctual, you smile. She's outrageous. She says things you never thought a woman would ever say.

You always knew what Grace was thinking and what she was going to say because she was so *nice.* You could predict her conversation like she was a good character on a soap opera. We never talked about sex. We just had it. It was okay, you know, Grace is a nice girl. Liz has a leather mask.

Liz has a *libido.*

Sometimes she ties me to the bed. That's not something you'd think you'd really go for 'cause it sounds a little kinky. The first time it was mentioned, you think, *Oh shit, I'm screwing a lunatic.* But then you look at Liz lying half-naked on your bed. Her nipples erect beneath a wet T-shirt. Her supple legs spread apart just enough so you can almost see. She's whispering. You know you're going to be her slave forever anyway. And then it's like the best. It lasts twice as long. You think you're going to die.

You think you're never going to have it this good ever again.

Take me.

Liz thinks so much and she puts meanings on everything that may or may not be the case and half the time I don't fucking know what she's talking about but she's got real nice breasts and a real sweet voice. But you have to remember to never say that to her when she's upset. She'll say you think of her as *an object* and then nothing you do will be right from that moment on.

Men are swine.

Liz is so good looking that she makes guys ache. I can see the guys gawking whenever we go anywhere. She sways a little too much when she walks. Guys make grunt sounds and sex noises when she passes by.

Liz has more orgasms than me.

I don't like taking her out to bars and things like that cause all the guys hit on her. They tell her they're going to *fuck* her and fuck her *right*. Like I'm a five-minute-wonder, pot-smoking, pea-brained pubescent who's never had it up before. They offer her all kinds of weird-ass shit. I've had the shit kicked out of me on more than one occasion. Guys just grab her.

"No harm in a feel," this one guy said.

Arsehole. We were dancing and he came up behind her and moved in for a squeeze. He groped my woman. The arsehole really groped her. His hands were on her breasts. And he kept going too.

"What's the big deal? I just want a touch."

Liz was shaking. She was trying to act like it was no big deal but he kept moving in toward her. He was real drunk. But no matter how I kept shoving him backward, he just kept coming back. Liz was standing behind me – holding onto my shirt – her fingers were trembling.

So, I decked him.

"Just *back off*, man."

"But you don't understand!"

"*Back off*, man."

"Don't get the wrong idea about me. I'm a good guy. Really. She's just a really good-looking woman and I'm a little drunk. Sorry. My girlfriend left me. You're just so pretty. Don't get the wrong idea. I'm a good guy."

He was a whiny bastard. Even after I pummelled him a few times in the face, he was still whining and saying that he didn't mean anything by it. I don't care if he meant *something* or meant *nothing*, he ain't supposed to grab a woman's tits. Who the hell cares what it means? If they ain't yours, don't touch them. Like I'm going to give a shit *why* he did it. He was whining through his blood. The bouncer let me hit him again when we dragged him outside. He was just snorting blood saying he did nothing wrong. He really thought he had a right to touch my woman's tits.

Brad.

"No one got hurt," he was whining.

Except maybe him.

Liz was ranting and raving. I remember what she kept saying to the bouncer: *people like that don't have basic logic skills*. I remember because it was odd. A man assaulted her and she's worried about his lack of mental capabilities. I know she studied logic. I know she has to think about the *greater* implications of everything. I know she has this *vision* of how things should be. I know all that. But I thought she would have felt something *personal*. I thought she would have cried.

I watched her closely after she blurted that statement. When the guy first grabbed her on the dance floor, I thought she was totally poised and unaffected. She had seemed so carefree as me and the bouncer dragged the guy outside.

But when I kept looking at her, I noticed the slight quivering in her lips and the clenched teeth. Her chin was tight. Her hands were wrapped tightly in little fists and that was when I noticed it. Her fists were not offensive, she didn't want to hit him. She was fighting *herself* – she was scared and she was scared to let me see that.

The bouncer understood or maybe he didn't. Maybe he was just so used to that kind of shit, he knew how to approach the situation. No doubt, he'd thrown guys out before and probably for worse shit. But when I looked at his face, his eyes were squinting, and there was a frown on his lips, I got the feeling that he did understand. Maybe not wholly, maybe not the way Liz felt, but he understood *something*.

I didn't.

Because I'm a simpleton.

"Hey pal," the bouncer told the guy. "If it's something you'd have to pay money for on the streets, then it ain't okay to just take it for free. Especially from someone who ain't selling."

The bouncer squeezed Liz's hand and told her everything would be okay. He looked at me for approval and then gave her a hug. He was a good guy. He patted her on the back like maybe he was her brother or something. She looked tiny in his arms. She was quiet. When he let her go, her face was a bit messy; her mascara had stained her eyes. But she was still stiff and her teeth were still clenched. He gave her a tissue and called a cab for us.

Cathy and her dolls.

The cab ride was silent. Just the beeps, hums and scrambled voices of other cab people coming through on the radio. The cab driver looked tired; he didn't say hello. But that was good. Liz wanted to be composed and the silence helped her. I stated our destination and then the ride was quiet.

When we got home, Liz went to the bathroom and cried. I never asked her what was wrong.

Menstruation.

Once a month, there is the *special* time in the household. Liz gets mad when you tell her she's pretty, she gets mad when you tell her she's smart, and she really gets mad when you tell her she's irritable. She gets mad when you tell her she's witty or funny or sensitive or anything really. She says she's not *a thing* and so she doesn't want to be labelled. When she's in this *female mood,* you can pretty much forget about saying most things. Nothing is politically correct when she's in the mood. And she asks the award-winning questions then, too.

If only I had a period, I might understand this hormone thing.

"If I looked different, would you still be with me?" she asked this one time. She enunciated. When she enunciates, you know you're in trouble. You replay everything you did in the last several hours to make sure you didn't ogle the woman at the pharmacy or that you didn't make fun of someone dropping milk or that you didn't kick the neighbour's dog. You have to establish that it is *the mood.*

"Eddy?"

She was staring a hole through me. I think she found an old birthday card from one of my exes. Normally, in that kind of situation, you panic. But she always tells me how she gets this *period* and how sometimes it makes her feel a little more *sensitive* ("bitchy" is more like it and that's still being politically correct) to comments and shit. So you don't panic. You relax. It's just her *period.* You think – *gross* (only you never never never tell her that even if she absolutely demands the absolute truth about what you think of her *cycle*). *Two days. Three – tops.*

"That's an interesting question, babe."

I didn't fall for it. I got her some more bunny-shaped chocolates and then I just kept drinking my beer. She kept *philosophizing*. When Liz gets going on a verbal tirade, it's like she finds *infinity*. It's interesting because she is so different and intelligent. She sees connections between things I never would have dreamed of, and it all makes sense. Sometimes, she's like a documentary on human beings on PBS.

On this day, she sat in the recliner for maybe an hour just ranting. (That's sort of normal for Liz. She reads way too much.) I kept giving her chocolates. I even made her hot cocoa and put some mini-marshmallows in it.

It's good that she can vent these things and it's good that I can be there for her when she has these needs. I'm her boyfriend, that's what I do. It's like I said, she's an interesting woman, and so it makes for good conversation. When Dakota is around and she hits one of those moods, then there are fireworks. They work on these things they call *problems* and *arguments*. And it's funny because it's not like our lives ever change even when they supposedly find the answers and discover these resolutions and *epiphanies*. But that sort of thing only happens when Dakota is around.

We're all the same. Liz still works at Lucy's Vintage, I still work at the super-absorbent paper factory, and Dakota is still an academic artist sponsored by tax money.

"Tell me, what do you think about men and the way they choose women partners, Eddy?"

When you're the only one in the room with a *sensitive* woman, you got to be a little careful. It's just that you got to be careful when you're talking back to her because you don't want to say anything like *your breasts are beautiful*. Then you're screwed. But it's like her breasts get bigger when she's all worked up like that. So, they are beautiful.

Her brow gets scrunched up, her nose is wrinkled and her lips are clenched tightly together. Like it hurts for her to be thinking. The pain is so clear in her face. I just want to pat her head and tell her everything will be okay only she'd never believe me.

"Have you ever noticed that some men have *types*? They have very specific types. They won't go out with tall women or all the women they date have blonde hair. What's your type, Eddy?"

Long hair, nice tits and makeup.

"Why do you generalize so much, Wren? Not all men are like that. I don't have a *type*. It's what the person is like that matters."

Correct that: long hair, nice tits *and not too much* makeup. Too much makeup is gross.

"Maybe you've never noticed your type, Eddy. I'm willing to bet if we look at pictures of all your ex-girlfriends, we'll find a blatant similarity."

Who needs makeup?

"Well, shit, there's probably *some sort* of similarity! I'm a guy. We're physical beings. We're *all* physical but it's like what I already said. It's what the person is like that matters. Cause I'm not with them anymore, am I? I'm with you, honey."

Grace never had tits and she cut her hair short but she didn't wear too much makeup.

"You're an odd fellow, Edward," Liz said. She calls me Edward whenever she's trying to start something because it's her *period* and she's feeling *sensitive*. "What did Grace look like?"

"Oh, she looked nothing like you, babe. She was kind of short and blonde. Frizzy hair."

"What did you see in her?"

Grace swallowed.

"She was, I don't know, funny and organized. I liked that. She always knew what was going on."

"You went out with a woman because she was *organized*?"

She never complained about not coming and she swallowed.

"She was pretty if that's what you're digging for. I'm not going to go out with someone I don't find attractive."

Unless it's a one-shot deal but even then.

Liz stared at me for a long time. I got warm. I got horny, too. But she was making me nervous. She was thinking. She was trying to figure something out. I felt like I was lying. I felt guilty. She just kept staring.

Then she got up and stood in front of me. She stared directly into my eyes. I got hard. She pulled her shirt off over her head – she was wearing this black push-up bra. Her breasts were heaving. They looked good enough to lick. Her nipples were hard and showing through the lace.

"You find me attractive?" she said.

You can't say anything at such a moment.

She pulled my shirt off and scratched her fingers across my chest. She unzipped my pants and went down. Holy fuck.

Liz.

Liz always smells good.

"That's what they call perfume, Eddy."

"Well, I guess all the other women can stop wearing perfume, because you've worn it to perfection."

That made Liz laugh.

She hates my stupid jokes, but she laughs at them.

Sometimes it looks like it's painful for her to laugh. And no matter how dumb the joke is, she always kisses me afterward. Just a little peck, but it's the little pecks that are comforting. It's like you know you're really with someone. When someone gives you a little peck kiss, you can almost hear them say, *dear.* Dakota and me bought some *Dumb Joke* books and *Even Dumber Jokes* books. When you got a good thing going, you don't want to lose it.

I always feel like we're just starting to date but we've been together for a long fucking time.

Liz:

Talking about the wild and wonderful adventures of his dick is one of Eddy's favourite pastimes. His dick has been everywhere and done everything. His dick should have a travelogue. When Eddy was just six years old, he had his first erection.

Eddy regales me with dick adventures even when I don't ask for them. Why would I ever want to hear that my boyfriend's dick has been engaged in extra curricular sexual activity? Sometimes I think he could talk about his dick forever. Sometimes I think he does. The only thing I really notice is that he has a *dick* – not a penis. Apparently, it's cuter when it's a dick or maybe when the *dick* strays, it's not really cheating either. Maybe if the *penis* had extracurricular sexual activity, it would count as unfaithful but since it's just the *dick*, it doesn't count.

Eddy loves my breasts only he calls them *tits.* Maybe the *tits* don't need to be faithful.

That's my third photograph for Eddy.

Penis.

It all began at his home in Halifax. His much older cousin Claire from a small town or village (he doesn't even remember the name of the place where she's from) had come to visit. He doesn't know how they're related exactly but he's certain it's not a blood tie so it wasn't incest although Eddy doesn't consider oral sex to be real sex anyway. Apparently, Claire was quite developed for her age and apparently Claire had a big crush on younger boys. Anyway, she took him out back and they climbed inside his father's Volkswagen beetle and she let him touch her breasts.

Eddy's convinced women stare at his crotch all the time, which is why he gets hard-ons frequently throughout the day. Eddy gets a hard on from thinking about other women and while thinking about how they brushed against him on the bus or smiled at him in the grocery store or passed him in the street not even noticing him. He says that doesn't make him unfaithful.

Fellatio. Cunnilingus.

He felt up our landlord's wife in the laundry room once – she wanted him so bad, he had to. Or so he says. He says her breasts are firm but her nipples are too dark. He says she grabbed him and says that doesn't count as being unfaithful to me because it was just a hand job. Apparently, what she really wants is to blow him.

"Is that okay?" he asked me.

You're breaking my heart.

"How am I supposed to answer that?"

"Well, do you mind? It's just oral."

"Do what you must," I said.

"It's not like it's being unfaithful."

Eddy always takes that as a *yes*. Each and every time Eddy has ever asked me one of these questions. I don't know what to call these types of questions, but he always takes my response as a yes. Perhaps it is a yes. Perhaps it is a yes. Perhaps I just don't give a shit anymore. Perhaps. I can't remember the last time we had good sex. Sex is good. Yeah, sex is good. I'd say *making love* but that feeling is long gone. It's just not even something that exists for other people in my little part of the world anymore. I don't think that even exists on earth two.

"It's just oral."

Eddy says I love to suck him off. He's sincere. He tells Dakota about it all the time. Eddy thinks I love his dick stuck in my tiny mouth like it's some kind of wonderful.

Used to be.

There's nothing wrong with oral sex. It's okay, but let's be realistic, it's not for the pleasure of the person doing it. I wouldn't call it orgasmic or anything truly sexual for that matter, but there's something intimate about it. Intimacy is the key. And within the intimacy, there lays love.

There had been intimacy. That was years ago, when I thought I was the only one. It was beautiful when it was us, when it was our little secret, when it was part of our romance, our personal sex life. When it was us.

Used to be everything and so much more.

I do it because he likes it. He's my boyfriend. Eddy. But he has this holier-than-thou attitude like I'm home all day waiting for this moment. I swear to God he thinks it's greater than sex.

Eddy has this sexual fantasy: he really wants to do it in my face and hair. I told him it would ruin my perm. He keeps telling me how *all* these *other* women did it for him. Like there's enticement – *be one of many, baby.*

"It's cheap and degrading," he said to me.

He thinks I'm cheap and degrading.

"Why do you want me to do something that you think is cheap and degrading?"

"Cause it excites me," he said.

"Then get a hooker to do it for you."

"Then it's not cheap."

I'm not even worth the price of a hooker.

"So I'm not even worth the price of a hooker?"

Eddy didn't have an answer for that question.

He never answers the referential questions. He leaves all the momentous occasions to a twilight-like silence. I can interpret my own answer although I know the meaning hidden within the silence but there is no answer. The other girlfriends struggled so hard to find an answer within his silence and each arrived at their own creation because in the end, Eddy's silence is his answer. There is no secret in his silence. Eddy merely lowers his eyes and pretends that perhaps I am secretly talking to myself, he just happened to overhear.

"Don't you want to make me happy?" he asked.

Eddy slammed my shoulder with a closed fist. It made my ears ring. Sometimes, he treats me like one of the guys. He prods and pokes me in the guts and fists my shoulders. But he jabs too hard and there are bruises all over my arm. He tells me to take vitamin E.

"It would be something different for us to try. What do you say, *baby*?"

Another act that doesn't make you unfaithful?

"I'm scared it will ruin my perm."

I don't even care if he believes me or not. I used to develop these long, elaborate and diplomatic excuses for when I didn't want to engage in his sexual fantasies but now I don't care. Apparently, they're all *jokes without punch lines*. Now I just say the first thing that comes to mind. I don't need a reason and I don't think he listens after I say "no" anyway. It probably all sounds the same to him anyway. He probably hates me.

Susan Farrell

Two monkeys listening to Al Green.

"Can't you get hair stuff that's resistant? I had a girl-friend with a perm before. She never had problems. She had a perm and I came on her. But she could never shut up, even when we were having sex. I think that's why I liked it so much, you know, she had to stop talking."

"*Maybe* I'll call her and ask her."

Eddy never noticed the sarcasm in my voice.

"I don't think I got her number now. But you know something? Like right after, I mean, *right after.* She starts whining 'kiss me'. Like she's all gross now."

Sometimes he says he's joking but I don't get the humour. I don't want to be one of his past girlfriends. I don't want to be a bad joke he tells to people. I don't want to be a whiny woman he wouldn't touch.

"So it's okay for her to have her face covered with your *stuff,* but it's not okay for you to *touch* any of it."

He just sat there, grinning like a true idiot.

"That's right."

"The woman you supposedly love just committed a very loving act for your sexual gratification and you wouldn't even touch her?"

"Made her shower first. Would you kiss her? That's gross."

"I see."

"So when can we do it, *baby*?"

I'd sooner watch him fuck a dead horse.

Eddy tells me that men are not obsessed with sex. He says it in his lecturing tone. I've never thought *men* are obsessed with sex. I just think Eddy is obsessed with sex. He masturbates with the underwear section of the Sears catalogue. And he gets hard whenever a woman wearing perfume gently brushes against him. It doesn't matter if she's unattractive. I know because he told me. He tells me weird things like this all the time because he says I don't judge him and so he can be this honest with me; he thinks it's great.

He thinks it is love.

Love.

Time for a beer.

Eddy says I have great legs. That will be my fourth photograph for Eddy.

There are times when I look at Eddy and he is so ugly that my eyes throb from the mere sight of him. It's like I cannot see him: his pale flesh, his blue eyes, the slightly curved nose (broken three times), the lower jaw that remains still whenever he speaks, the muscular arms and the lean shoulders, his familiar beer gut (that he's working on). I see none of that. I can't even see his adoring and horny smile. I see the stories of all the miserable and wretched things he has ever done to other women.

Used to be.

I imagine him holding a perfume bottle, jerking off in his bathroom cubicle, with his jeans wrapped around his feet because he's too lazy to take them completely off, desperately imagining the face of the last blonde woman who brushed against him in the bus. I see him getting mad when he can't remember the finest lines in the corners of her face and the sudden lack of memory makes him limp and then he has to start rubbing frantically to get the action going again. And he gets frustrated. Like it's a chore to give himself pleasure.

Used to be.

He likes to do it right next to the shower stall so he can press his forehead against the towel rack. The towel gets wet and it smells of sex. I always tell him to do it in the shower. He never cleans up his mess.

There can be only one.

"Why don't you clean it up?" he asked me.

"Why don't you?"

"You're the woman, baby."

"What is that supposed to mean?"

"Now don't get all hoity-toity, Jesus, you always think there's something wrong with the things I say. I didn't mean nothing by it. I was just saying, you could clean it up."

"It's your *stuff*."

"Yeah, like you never had it in your mouth before."

"You're disgusting."

He laughed.

Eddy laughs whenever I call him disgusting. Apparently, Eddy told Dakota my special nickname for him was "disgusting." Apparently, Dakota told Eddy I was being cute. Apparently, Dakota thinks "disgusting" is endearing. Let's ask Dave.

Dakota is quite possibly the biggest fucking lying asshole I have ever met; he is a smooth-talking whore and I can't understand why women keep falling in love with him. He tells lie after lie; the man will say whatever he has to say to get a woman to fuck him. His words have no meaning. Literally.

I cannot possibly recollect how many times he has told a woman that he has fallen in love at first sight and the woman believes him. Dakota has "been" in the film industry, the military, the music industry, and the stock market.

There is not one girlfriend who did not confide in me that she *secretly* knew she was his one and only, even though his longest relationship to date is four months. This, she knew in less than four months. I've known Dakota for perhaps five years. And there has never been one girlfriend that I ever even suspected might be his one and only.

Summertime makes me feel good.

The heat made it impossible to move without sweating. Little droplets of sweat formed with just the slightest movement. Most of the summer vacation to the interior found us melting on the front veranda.

"Why does it make me a bad guy if women are stupid?" Dakota asked me.

"People aren't stupid if they believe in love," I said. "People aren't expecting a liar."

We sweltered in the heat. We were attempting to prepare for a barbecue; Eddy was prodding the charcoal, Dakota and me were having beer. Eddy's little brother Dave and Dakota's latest girlfriend had walked down to the lake to skip rocks; Dave's girlfriend never came with us.

"I mean, if women are willing to fall for stupid lines, why am I the bad guy? They *choose* to believe they can *change* me."

"You lie," I said. "Take your little girlfriend right now. Have you told her you're so in love, you see yourself marrying her already?"

Dakota cleared his throat.

"Yeah, I said that," he said.

"Is it true?"

Sipping his beer, he sat down on the railing. He had nothing else to say. His new girlfriend and Dave were visible through the trees; they were still skipping rocks in the lake. Eddy couldn't hear us; he was too busy fumbling with the barbecue.

"No," Dakota said. "I don't *dislike* her. She's a nice girl, but that won't get me laid."

"Whatever gets you through the night," I said.

"But you don't respect me."

From the shore, we heard Dave ecstatic with laughter. He had already had a few too many. He nearly fell into the lake, but the new girlfriend managed to grab his arm; they tumbled onto the shore.

"Barbeque is ready!" Eddy announced.

The conversation ended until later in the evening, when we were cooling off.

"I still think the women prefer the lies," Dakota said. "See, that way, they can have casual sex and then just say the guy was an ass who lied to them."

As Dakota made his retarded statement, he cast a furtive glance at Dave as if for moral support. Dave puffed up importantly; he was treasuring the fact that Dakota was *sharing* this moment with him. Dave would endorse the conviction of anyone who would give him approval.

"You're still a liar," I said.

"But you think I'm taking advantage of these women and I'm just trying to point out that *these* women want to be taken advantage of. I have said I'm not a *relationship* kind of guy. I tell them it's not going to *be* anything serious. They know right from the start. They must be attracted to the way I am."

"Oh come on, Liz, say something," Dave said.

Eddy stepped onto the veranda with a cooler of beer. He unscrewed the lids off a few beers and passed them to us. He mouthed, I *love you* to me and gave me a knowing glance about Dakota.

But Dakota saw; he watched the whole exchange with an intense scrutinizing gaze, normally he never watched me and Eddy.

His face.

Dakota was still, like an abstract painting, for a moment. He looked artificial. I remember. The fine lines in his face grew cold and hard and his mouth seemed carved and aesthetically chosen. An incisive glare in his eyes insinuated he was abandoned in some repressed memory that had perhaps surfaced in the chill of the wind as it ruffled his cotton shirt. His face flushed when he realized I had seen his countenance of despair.

"I think a lot of these women only go out with me for the novelty, you know. They get to take a Mi'kmaq home to Mommy and Daddy. They use my *promiscuity* as a justification to break up with me. What would they *do* if I were a commendable guy? They'd have to have a *real* relationship with me."

"I'm sorry you feel that way," I said.

"And for me," he said. "The promiscuity is a defence because it doesn't hurt as much to think they're leaving me because I'm just an ass when it comes to relationships. Assholes don't deserve love. Natives do."

"You never give anyone a chance to prove you wrong."

Eddy and Dave watched us like we were a talk show.

"Would you have a real relationship with an Indian, Liz?" he asked.

He stared squarely into my eyes with a stark daring provocation. His pupils were dilated. I did not break the stare. Eddy was snickering in the background. Dave was muttering to himself about being confused. Dakota clenched his jaw tightly; the blue in his veins intensified.

"Would you?" he asked me again. Eddy stiffened as he poked the charcoal in the barbecue. He didn't want me to answer the question.

What I didn't know at the time was that this particular act, which Dakota performed in front of me many times, was also a lie. Dakota had determined that I was the type of woman who would be susceptible to a man in despair. Apparently, I am the type of person who doesn't like to see anyone get a raw deal. As Nina said, sometimes you meet someone so you can learn something about yourself.

Adam.

Adam smelled like new leather and Christmas and his brow was always furrowed. He wore only plain white T-shirts and he had an unlined notebook with him wherever he went so he could capture any fleeting thoughts. He thought women would never be interested in him if he wore his silver-rimmed rounded glasses, but then he realized it was never women he wanted to attract anyway.

Someday, I'll tell Eddy my first love was actually a gay man and then he'll finally stop being jealous of the past. Someday, I'll do that.

Adam and I lived together for two years although, in the end, it felt more like a few decades.

"I did," I said.

Dakota smiled.

Eddy opened a few more beers.

There was a full moon that night. Crickets were singing. There were owls and other night noises, including the snoring of Dakota's latest girlfriend, who had already passed out for the night. It was peaceful.

Dakota did not address me for the rest of the evening. He was quiet and somewhat withdrawn – curled up near the railing of the veranda with his head cocked toward the stars. He didn't even partake in the asinine conversation about extra-buttered popcorn and action movies and kickboxing that seemed to so enthral Eddy and his hyena of a brother.

"How much balance do you think you'd have to have to kick a guy three times in a row?" Dave asked excitedly.

"Are you kicking him high or low?"

"High."

"You'd never get three kicks in anyway because the guy would react. He'd knock you down. It's an ineffective way to fight."

Pissing off the side of the veranda.

"So, hey? The only *thing* about this place," Dave said. He had had about fifteen beers by this time. "The *problem*. Like, you know, coming to the cabin, is – there are no girls, right? There's nowhere to get some girls. Aw, man. *Girls*."

"We got Liz."

I heard Eddy's cold slurred voice cut through the stillness of the night as his tongue wrapped around the syllable of my name and it made me nauseated. His statement bounced around my mind, but I kept my head lowered and focused on my crossword book. It was just one of his tasteless jokes that he would, no doubt, apologize profusely for later. The veranda squeaked beneath the shifting weight of Dakota as he swirled about on the steps. Another beer opened.

Another beer opened.

Eddy crooned my name.

"Hey, Liz."

When I think of romance, I think of my lover crooning my name on a moonlit night. I think of open golden fields with carefree breezes, flowing gowns of white silk, and icy rainstorms with thunder and lightening. I think of the Gothic era – stone castles with cold corners and dark shadows, whispered echoes of love that carry on to infinity, intricately carved gargoyles with portentous eyes and deformed poets with bitter bleeding hearts.

That's what I think of.

What I have is Eddy.

Eddy.

Eddy. The love of my life is an arsehole.

When he has his nightmares, Eddy sleeps with his head resting against my breasts and I quote poetry, he tells me he's proud of my intellect. He calls me *Wren* and nibbles on my ear then snuggles until he's comfortable and falls asleep. He calls me *Wren*. It's affectionate, but I have no idea why and at this point in our relationship, I can't let him know I don't know the significance of his term of endearment.

A softer pillow than my heart.

"Hey Liz, Lizzie. Lizzer. Lessee." Eddy slurred.

He was loud and his words grew more and more garbled. I didn't answer him so he got louder and then louder. Standing like a wild man in love, he began shouting my name. My name echoed over the lake; it could have sounded like some Byronic proclamation of eternal passion, but instead it sounded like a drunken arsehole forgetting something at the grocery store.

"Liz! Lizzie!"

Another beer and another beer opened. Dakota's hand lightly brushed against my cheek and his breath warmed my ear.

"Liz," he whispered softly. "Just answer him."

I don't know why I listened to Dakota. Eddy would have forgotten me in another moment anyway – he would have grown fascinated with the sound of his own voice as it carried across the lake and echoed in the darkness. I would have been just another object on the veranda.

"What, Eddy?" I asked.

"Take your shirt off and show Dave your titties."

I was more amazed that he managed to utter the statement than anything else. When I glared at him – propped against the rail post for support, dripping beer in one hand and a skipping rock in the other – I knew he was hard. This was one of his greatest pubescent fantasies developed late at night in his little bedroom under the covers while staring at cheap porn magazines because he didn't have enough money to get the more expensive ones. He was showing off his woman to his pathetic brother.

"Give him a little feel, too."

It will be our little secret.

Eddy was laughing. He was so damn sure that he had just made the best joke ever. Part of me wanted to rip my shirt off and see how funny he'd find his statement then. Who would be laughing at his little joke then? And I'd be able to say *You told me to do it*. Dave stood before me making pinching motions with his hands and slurping sounds with his mouth. He swirled his tongue about in his mouth. Dakota's hand pressed against mine. He squeezed but only for a moment. He handed me a beer.

"Just enough to get him off," Eddy persisted. He wasn't even looking at any of us anymore; he was lost in his own malediction. Thrilled with his own licentious behaviour; like perhaps he thought he was the first individual to get aroused by desecrating actions, he laughed. He was still howling about my breasts, his brother and something about cocks and strange *philosophies* that he felt justified such actions.

Eddy was a born comedian.

Dakota gingerly leaned forward, slightly between the drunks and me. Tossing his sweater across my legs, he rested an arm against me. He took a lengthy drink from his beer. I could hear him breathing heavily. He was blocking me from them.

"Let's see them perky tits. Bounce them around."

"You are disgusting," I said.

Eddy thought I was joking.

Eddy always thinks I'm joking and perhaps I am. Perhaps I am joking. Perhaps the whole thing is a joke. Perhaps it's all very funny. Perhaps my whole life is a pathetic joke. Perhaps it's just a joke and the punch line is yet to come. Perhaps it's the best joke ever told in humanity. Perhaps I just don't have a sense of humour anymore.

Yeah, I think that's it. That's it. That's the problem.

Perhaps that is the fucking problem.

It's just oral.

I said no once. I think I said no. I don't want him to fuck anyone but me. I don't want him to fuck anyone but me. Is that so much to want? He's my lover. My best friend – he's supposed to be mine and mine alone. That's what *everyone* says – that's what the infamous *everyone* says. I'm Eddy's and he's mine. That's the big promise they tell you when you're little.

When you're little, no one tells you you're one and only is going to be adulterous. No one says that.

Eddy cheated on me, which apparently wasn't real cheating since it was oral sex, and then he got mad at me. He said I didn't *trust* him, that I didn't do *something* for him. He never made sense. He cheated, and apparently, it was my fault.

When he was finished his tantrum about my tits, he started drinking yet another beer. The only thing I could hear was his slurping; he was drinking another beer. I could feel the rage inside me growing like a tiny little ball. And I said,

"Go fuck your stupid whore."

And he sort of lunged toward me, but Dakota sat up straight.

"What are you sitting there for?"

"Why don't you have some water, man?" Dakota said.

Perhaps the problem is right in front of me.

Our summer vacation to the interior was just A-plus. Talk about a romantic proposal. Lucky me.

7. Perception.

How well do you know your partner, both physically and emotionally? How much do you feel you know about this particular partner and do you feel that you need to know more?

Eddy:

Liz was sort of a virgin.

A white wedding.

When I first met Liz, she had never really been with anyone. She was a wicked bad flirt. Her eyes said, *Come fuck me.*

The homemade beer was not tasty. Dakota and I were all at some "back to university" party; he was trying to pick up some first-year chicks and I was trying to get drunk.

Sitting in an easy chair near the bar was this gorgeous woman. She was in red. Dakota and me had already checked her out earlier. She was with a few others, they all looked like freaks. You know the type – their shirts were a little too small and the collars were a little too big. Everything was made of polyester with bright flashy designs and colours. They wore bell-bottoms, only they weren't real bell-bottoms, they were modern and updated and that made them look tackier. You just know they thought they were original and if you told them it had all been done in the seventies already, they wouldn't believe you. Pompous airbags.

Talk like a smart-ass.

Dakota and me had seen her around at all sorts of parties; she was always a fixture in the background. We'd look for her. This fucking gorgeous woman in short leather skirts or tight leather pants and short shirts that let her belly button show. Her hair was always loose, hanging over her shoulders. She looked like she should have been in a shampoo commercial.

When she walked across the room, heads turned. You could hear guys mouthing off about her. She swayed when she walked – her shoulders fell back and she held her arms so delicately – she had these long beautiful fingers. There was a bit of bounce in her breasts and then there were her blue eyes. She had that look – *that look* – in her eyes.

You always wanted to be the one why she had *that* look in her eyes. You always wanted to be the one telling the stories or maybe you wouldn't. Maybe you would just smile and keep it to yourself, knowing you were the one with the truth and they were the ones lying. Maybe you'd do something like beat the living shit out of those lying bastards for making up such bitter shit about a beautiful woman. Just because they could. And just because you could.

Slut.

Dakota said she was the most beautiful woman he had ever laid eyes on. He said,

"She is the greatest woman I'll ever have the privilege of meeting."

You remember something like that 'cause it almost makes him sound like he already met her even though you know he never did. Or so you think.

I don't recall, Mr. Senator.

Dakota says now that he never said that and if he did, he was drunk. But that don't matter none because he's drunk half his whole life anyway. That would mean nothing he says has any meaning. You know he said it. You remember hearing the words come from his mouth. It's the kind of thing you'd be worried about except you know she thinks he's more repulsive than horse manure.

Everyone thought Liz was easy because she always had a drink in her hand, but she always arrived alone and no one ever saw her leave with anyone. She just looked too good to be a virgin. I watched her chew up a man once.

One guy with a shaved head, horn-rimmed glasses and a T-shirt that said, *I fuck libertines* was entertaining everyone with his sheer brilliance.

Conservatism this.

Neo-political that.

Postmodern something right up my ass.

"It's not possible for a woman to get raped by a man," this guy said. Apparently, there was no room for a *biology* course in his liberal arts education. "That's a big fallacy. Just one more lie to keep *the man* down. Women work out now.

The average man needs a weapon to rape a woman. I don't think rape occurs half as much as they say it does."

"So you're claiming the statistics are fabricated?" Liz said.

It was slow motion. He kind of turned and looked at her like he thought no one would ever question him. He didn't look too impressed when he saw Liz. He looked like he wanted to fuck her and get it over with.

"I'm saying most rapes are not *rape*. It's when the woman feels regret in the morning and changes her mind."

"Oh, I see your problem," Liz said. "You're having some comprehension difficulty. You're not grasping what the civilized world refers to as *concepts*. You don't know what *rape* is. There are three different *concepts* here – rape, sex and regret. Rape and sex are physical acts and regret is a feeling. Three separate issues. You think *rape* is *sex*. I think you need to read the dictionary, boy. Sex is a consensual act between persons. Rape is a violent assault."

He stared. He stared and there was this dumb-ass look on his face. Like he had just said two and two is four and someone told him he was wrong. His face got all tight and the headache was visible in his eyes. His glasses fogged up; he spilled his dry white wine in the lap of his periwinkle pants. He was mad. People were laughing.

"Fabulous one," some chick told Liz. The chick was wearing a plush white jumpsuit. She caressed Liz's bare arm and the two giggled softly against each other's bare necks.

Dakota thought she was awesome. He was squirming in his chair so much; you'd think he'd never seen a woman before.

Dakota always gets his woman.

"Unless," Liz continued, "even on a practical level, you don't know what sex is and when you're on a date, this confusion comes into play. And you can't quite figure out why the women are always crying and freaking out on you. What exactly do you do on a date?"

The retro crowd was laughing.

Dakota was on fire. He stood up so he could get a better look at the debate between Liz and the guy with the glasses. Dakota was wholly focused on Liz. His eyes traced her outline over and over again.

"I love that woman," he muttered.

The guy with the horn-rimmed glasses never answered her; he just sort of smiled sarcastically. Dakota was mumbling something about her brilliance and footnotes in history books or something like that. I was watching her silver medallion. It kept sliding between her breasts. Her friend kept touching her and brushing up against her.

All the guys wanted her.

Desire.

I thought I saw her look at me.

Dakota.

Dakota wanted her; they seemed to look at each other. Through the bobbing heads and all the drunken spitting laughter and the entire phoney mingling, their eyes locked tight. They had that look – that look that says they know each other.

Liz is the type of girl that you think you're never going to get, cause she's so fucking good looking and smart and funny and she's so *together*. You think she's never going to look at a simple ass like you cause she could have any man. People were thanking her when she made that comment. You got someone like Dakota, who can sweet-talk anyone, so why should you even get in the race?

Drunk.

Liz was two sheets to the wind when she walked up to me at one of those parties. It was a mid-winter party. Her big blue eyes were all glossy and there was a bit more of a swank in her walk than usual. Her breathing was heavy, like she had to concentrate real hard. She touched my face. And just maybe a part of you was freaking out because *this* woman was actually approaching you. But you maintained your confidence.

"You spilled something," she whispered.

She let me lick her fingers and that was pretty much when I decided I was taking her home and screwing her until it hurt. There's a part of me that thinks I didn't care if she even told me her name and there's another part of me that thinks I loved her right then and there.

A fuck is a fuck.

"You're shy," she said.

"I've seen you around. You were at Amber's party last week. I was trying to catch your eye. You hardly ever talk to anyone. You're just always here with that guy from the Creative Writing department."

"I find it hard meeting new people." I said.

"You're doing all right with me," she said. "I'm Liz."

Cause I'd do anything to fuck you.

She smiled and when she laughed, she brushed against my side and held onto my arm with her hand. She was wearing lots of silver rings and bracelets. She was soft. The metal was cold. I could smell her. She smelled like strawberries and her hair looked shiny like silk. She reminded me of Christmas and I didn't even know why.

Then that guy with the horn-rimmed glasses sort of approached us. He had a bit of hair this time. He kept sneaking glances at us, staring between his comments (which no doubt were very poignant and clever). And then real quiet-like, Liz moved in closer to me.

Tight shirt.

Her bright and bubbly face fell flat and even her touch suddenly felt cold. Liz looked pale; she was watching him. You don't always know what someone is thinking when their face gets that blank look. She could have been thinking anything: she could have been too drunk, she could have been thinking about a drive home, the last thing she ate, paying her phone bill, or what was on TV. She could have been thinking about the guy in the horn-rimmed glasses.

It was him.

She was thinking about him. She was tracing harsh circles with her hands on the rim of her beer stein. Her knuckles were chalky white with tension. Her eyes were sharp and piercing and her lips had lost all of the sexy poutiness – she was stiff all over. Like the way animals get in front of headlights.

Most guys would have left her now – thinking she was hooked on him, thinking they had totally lost their chance of scoring, thinking they'd have to try elsewhere – thinking she was a lost cause. But you could just tell the way she was thinking about him wasn't romantic or sexual – it was something else. You could tell by her eyes. She *was* thinking of him. But I wasn't discouraged because the look on her face said she wasn't fantasizing about something warm and comforting. She was thinking of a nightmare.

We were both quiet.

Hollow eyes.

Smirking, he turned and cast a glance at Liz. His face was bright and bold and everything her face was not. He didn't look at me; he kept his eyes focused on Liz. Then, he oozed his tongue out and licked his lips. He cocked his head and raised a brow. He blew her a kiss.

Liz was frozen. Putting my arms around her, we left together.

They were on the floor by the coffee table, in front of the TV.

Dakota was talking his big talk and she was reduced to a fascinated child with wide eyes; I knew it was going to be a long boring Saturday afternoon. It was raining like always. They were doing a crossword together. It was from the newspaper that I bought for our morning breakfast. Dakota showed up almost immediately after we cleared the dishes. Obviously, he didn't get lucky that night. I was watching the sports news.

"The world would be better off if we all used Shakespearean English, don't you think?" Dakota asked her.

"I think we'd have more misunderstandings."

"No more than we already have now."

"True. True."

She was so enthralled, you think about what she's going to say later. You hear her saying how much she loathes his very being. You hear her say it every time he leaves the house. It's the first thing she utters whenever he leaves. She's sociable with him for your sake – that's what she always says. She's got class and tact. It always makes you feel good when she says it. But you can always see the way the colour in her cheeks flush when he's around and he says all these clever little things that you can never think of.

But can he lick his own eyeballs like a gecko lizard?

They laughed together. Their bodies leaned in close and collided because it was just so darn witty. I must have been laughing somewhere in my subconscious. I was just repressed to feel it. Yeah, that's what it must have been. Liz giggled in her sweet little girl way; back to her wicked flirtatious ways when she wore the leather pants and acted like a feisty wench who needed taming. You'd think she'd never heard anything funny before. You'd think she was single.

You'd think lots of things if you were a paranoid kind of guy but when you got a whoremonger for a best friend, you have to think of these things. When you got a woman like Liz who can drink you under the table and she gets freaking horny and insecure when she's drunk, you got reason to think – *maybe*.

Insecure and horny. There can't be a worse combination. The whole thing just kind of gives you something to think about.

Dakota told me he'd never do my woman.

Where is my woman now?

Sometimes you think you know things even when people don't even tell you out loud. There's a lot more to communication than the words you hear. You think you know and that's enough because that's more than you should know anyway. You don't need to hear it to know it and embrace it as a truth; you can just accept it in a quiet kind of way. If you were meant to know something, then somebody would tell you. Until that day, I'm a content man.

Everyone's got a nightmare they don't need to share.

Just one spot of darkness.

Liz had a nightmare – that was all I needed to know. All her fierce independence disappeared like maybe it had never really been there to begin with. She was just pale, pasty and uncertain. I held her hand.

"Can I have your number, Liz?" I asked her.

Liz said I'm shy.

Shy.

Liz says the only reason I asked for her number rather than taking her home for the night is because I'm shy. She says I was scared of *being rejected*. She says I was *insecure*. But you know, when a woman puts her fingers in your mouth, rejection isn't exactly a big fear. You worry about other things like maybe is it your birthday and your best friend hired a call girl or something. That would be the only thing you'd worry about.

You ask for a woman's number when you want more than just free fun. Besides, we slept together the next night anyway.

"There's a case of beer missing," Dakota shouts.

"Eh?"

"I say, an entire case of my special beer is missing," he says. "It was in the fridge. Did you take it in the crapper with you?"

Liz:

Eddy says I have a cute ass. Between smacking it and pinching it, my ass is always bruised or so it seems. My cute ass.

That will be my fifth photograph for Eddy.

Adam smelled like citrus vodka as I entered his studio loft. He had been drunk for days on end only he called it a *period of creativity*. Pulling some of his folders from a shelf, he asked if I wanted to see some of his latest artistic pieces. He was jubilant; he said they were for me.

A large spectacular canvas was mounted on his studio loft wall. This painting was dedicated to me. It was titled, *Love.* The painting was streaks of soft-coloured paint on a white canvas – the paint was thick and heavy like congealed cream – it was difficult to see the lines. It looked like milky opals and candy.

"Love is as close to God as we will ever be," he told me. "It is our purest emotion and our saving grace and its origin is in superficiality and selfishness. How ironic."

I laughed.

"You called my painting 'Love'," I said.

"I did love you," he said. "I do love you."

He just didn't want to be with me.

"Love is a little fragment of every emotion available to the human being. Each fragment alone is insignificant and can be dangerous in and of itself but when all these fragments are drawn together, we have unity – beauty – we have *love*. Love is all encompassing – a spectrum of emotion. It is the unified whole of the rainbow. It is the conglomerate. Like the spectrum, it is all colours woven together... And when all colours of the spectrum are woven together – white. Love is white," he told me.

"Come," he said. "Have a drink with me. Sit."

Sounding like a B-grade actor and looking like a weary world traveller, he told me the intimate details of the emotional break-up with his last boyfriend – some exotic dancer at one of the gay clubs downtown. He had been quite fond of this most recent boyfriend.

"He had a winning sense of humour, Liz," he said. "It's a shame you never met him. He was sweet."

"Perhaps you two can still work it out," I said.

Rolling his eyes, yet exploring the possibility of reconciliation, Adam sighed. He squeezed my hand as he spoke.

"How was your trip in the interior? What god-forsaken little spot in the middle of nowhere did Eddy take you?" Adam asked.

"Eddy proposed," I said.

All eye contact ceased.

"He wants to get married and have kids," I said. The words were timid whispery sounds – they seemed not even audible inside my own head. It was a wonder Adam could hear them.

Huis Clois.

Reaching across the table, Adam squeezed my hand.

"You've never told him then," he said.

Opening my mouth to speak, I found I could say nothing. Instead, I cried. Gently pushing me aside, he slid onto the chair with me, enveloping me within his arms, and kissed the top of my head repeatedly.

"Talk to me," Adam whispered. He repeated himself only I no longer knew what it was I wanted to say. The thoughts had passed or maybe the thoughts hadn't set yet. Maybe the cement was still wet inside my mind. Heavy and wet. Dragging me down. Deeper and deeper.

Adam was calling my name softly.

There will be no little Eddys running around, at least, not from me.

"How long did you live with your first boyfriend?" Eddy asked.

"I don't know exactly," I said. "Almost two years, I guess."

Eddy wanted to know about my relationship with Adam, *but not really*. He found a poem Adam wrote for me, and he asked a few questions. If I told him that Adam is gay, then he would want to know why I stayed with him for so long and then he would have to know about the dead uterus.

"He lives here, right?" he asked.

I saw him the other day.

It's almost as if Eddy thinks I was a virgin when we met. He wants to know he is my only love, but when I talk of Adam there is still love in my voice and he can hear it. But he's hearing the wrong kind of love. If Adam hadn't loved me then. If he hadn't been there for me. But Eddy is too stubborn to listen after that anyway. He becomes a quiet boy who denies everything – he's *not upset, he's not angry, he's not even jealous, he doesn't care.*

"We have to get ready, your friends will be here," I said. "Didn't you say you wanted to fix your goatee?"

Immediately, he jumped up and headed into the washroom. The goatee, his prized accomplishment, had been the object of his obsession for a few weeks.

The party began.

We had parties all the time. Nothing really happens at these parties; they all feel the same: beer, rum or whiskey with hockey, baseball or football. Some of the guys. A couple of cheap sluts. *Fuck this. Fuck that.* The object that is getting fucked depends on the season. This party happened to be a beer and baseball event and everyone was fucking politicians.

"Politicians don't give a shit about people," Dakota said. "You don't get into politics because you're a humanitarian. You get into politics because you want power. *Fuck that.*"

"Fucking politicians," Dave said.

At least Dave was finally fitting in.

In the centre of the room, and the centre of our lives, was the television. The volume was ear-splitting. Similar to church, we were all seated about the TV, listening to its message. There was a war being broadcast on TV; the coverage kept interrupting the baseball game until Eddy managed to find a channel that was not featuring the war. Popcorn was exploding in the kitchen.

Dakota's young woman of the week was breathing heavily in the bathroom – she was on the verge of vomiting. As usual, I was the only other woman present so I had to see her.

She was *Amber.*

"I think I'm going to be sick!"

Amber, a first-year acting student from the film school, wasn't that smart. It was all very emotional.

"I am so in love with him," she told me as she sat on the bathroom floor. "He's just misunderstood."

Yeah.

Smiling, I gave her a towel and cleaned her up. She was fine; she was probably just nervous since she was meeting Dakota's friends for the first time and this was a *real* relationship for her.

Amber was wearing pink plastic heels, which were hollowed out to display a picture of a gold fish, but she couldn't walk in them and after she had finished several beers, she could scarcely walk at all. Dakota had to wait on her because she had to have more beer – she *just might* still say no to him.

Amber, who could not have been more than nineteen, despite being so in love with Dakota, began flirting with Eddy.

She was a tawdry collection of skin and bones with fake tits wrapped tightly in fuchsia coloured polyester – too much make-up and a boy's haircut, which was supposed to be cute like Liza Minnelli back in the day, I suppose. She looked like an elf on oestrogen. Her belly button was pierced twice and she wore flowered hip-huggers to display her belly loops. She fancied herself a poet, but she had never heard of Pound or Atwood or Eliot or Byron or Yeats; she thought Shakespeare was a scientist and a sonnet had something to do with thunder. Dakota met her at one of his live word events in some condemned building somewhere on Commercial Street.

Cheap slut number seventeen.

I'm going to change him.

"I take singing lessons at the Women's Perspective Theatre in Point Grey."

"That sounds great," I told her. She giggled like perhaps she was flirting with me as well; it must be nice when everything is sexual. Both of Eddy's eyebrows rose when she squeezed my thigh as thanks for my ridiculously supportive comment regarding her singing.

"How *sumptuous*."

That was Amber's little phrase. If I heard it once that night, I heard it a thousand times. She pronounced the "p" a little too much and usually spit on Eddy.

"Ha," Eddy said. "You spit on me a little."

They both laughed. The three of us were sitting on the sofa together. Eddy. The girl flirting with Eddy. Me. Despite the fact that on any other occasion, I may have met her as someone's younger sister and liked her, by the end of the evening I even loathed the way she breathed.

"How *sumptuous*."

"You really think so?" Eddy asked. He tilted toward her, placed his hand on her thigh and squeezed ever so effortlessly. He gazed into her eyes, she blushed, and I was nauseated.

I was dying to ask him what "sumptuous" meant. I was dying to say that Eddy and I were living together.

Did she want to keep flirting with him? Could she ask him to use Toilet Duck?

"So you think my idea is good?" he asked. He was beaming.

"Oh, yes, yes, yes, for sure," she said. "It's like, you just, so know what you're doing. Right? Like a lot of people, you know, just don't and that's, like…. You know what I mean. It's sumptuous." She giggled, blushed even, at all of his half-assed jokes, and fixed her lipstick constantly by gazing at her reflection in the wine glass. She thought it was more lady-like to drink her beer in a wine glass.

I was drinking my beer with a straw.

Eddy was acting like he owned the whole world.

"Anyone want another one while I'm up?"

I stopped drinking; Eddy didn't. When the party was over, I cleaned up the kitchen while Eddy munched on potato chips. He plopped onto the sofa; he lay there for a long time, just watching me, asking me to undress slowly and babbling about something tedious. He kept grabbing my wrist – he wanted me to straddle him. He said he was in the mood for some *sumptuous* loving. I wondered if I spit on him, would he think it was *cute*.

And he passed out.

His chin is not shaped for a goatee.

His hand was still on his chin, touching the stubble, he was like a babe with his favourite toy. Walking into the bathroom, I unplugged his electric shaver, returned to the living room and shaved the whole damn thing off. It was a close shave. It was a good shave, but then again I had gotten him the best shaver money could buy – in my budget.

In the morning, Eddy awoke and went for his jog.

We sat at the kitchen table, drank our coffee, ate our toast and read the morning paper together like we always did. He kissed me on the cheek before he went to work.

"I love you," Eddy said. "You know there will never be anyone but you, right?"

Yes, only me. And the landlord's girlfriend, and of course, the occasional girl who flirts with him at a party because as everyone knows, flirting is healthy for a relationship.

Romance.

Romance became sex on a Monday afternoon three Valentine's ago at quarter past six in the evening. I remember because I was lying in Eddy's queen-sized bed, wearing a red satin teddy with spaghetti straps, sipping Kahlua from a plastic wine glass. Alone. I watched the red numbers on the digital clock radio change minute by minute until I finally gave in and turned on the TV. After all, it didn't matter.

Time would continue regardless of whether or not I watched TV. Eddy had forgotten our anniversary and that wasn't going to change regardless of whether or not the television was on or off. The sitcoms numbed my frustration.

Time.

Time and *waiting* were irreconcilable adversaries. And quarter past six became six thirty and six thirty became seven – seven-thirty – eight – eight-thirty – nine – and then at ten o'clock, Eddy and I had sex for thirty-three minutes.

"Why didn't you just call me?"

You're supposed to remember.

"Why didn't you just call me?"

You're supposed to remember.

"If you want something special, you got to tell me."

I thought he'd remember, maybe even *anticipate*, our anniversary especially since it's Valentine's Day. I thought all the posters and advertisements in the newspapers and magazines and on TV would jog his memory. I thought he'd never forget since the general persons of society commemorate our day. I thought he would remember but I would be wrong.

"You know, Wren, guys aren't good with remembering things like that."

He has yet to forget a hockey game.

He has yet to forget anything work-related.

He has yet to forget anything Dakota plans.

He has yet to forget.

Perhaps I should have called him. Perhaps it is all my fault. Perhaps it is childish of me to expect him to remember Valentine's Day. Perhaps sentimentality is just one more ideal I must release to the world of mythology, to the world of dreams, to the childhood vision of the great humanity in the sky. Eddy and I met on a Valentine's Day. And our romance began on a Valentine's Day. It is quite befitting that our sex also began on a Valentine's Day. Perhaps I should just accept the differences between the genders, maybe some DNA testing will be able to alleviate this selective memory Eddy believes men have as a result of their biology. Eddy says he doesn't remember important dates. But what he means is he doesn't remember *girlfriend important* dates. Everything else he remembers. He feels free to forget about me because I'm special and he loves me. I can see how it all makes sense.

"You should have just called. I was just with the guys – we were all just sitting around having a few beers, just doing nothing really. I would have come over. I didn't realize you were here. It's not like you told me you were coming or something."

"Don't worry about it."

He knows it's a lie; I know it's a lie. Perhaps we should talk about it for twenty minutes and watch ourselves scramble for verbal pieces of diplomacy and tact because we believe lies are solvable puzzles offering insights to humanity. We believe lies are meant to be cracked open so the truth oozes out like a great reward. But that's not what lies are: lies are small graces that get us through the night. Lies are carefully crafted masks to protect the glass-like fragility of our souls.

"Don't worry about it, Eddy."

And so, we kissed and had sex for another thirty-three minutes. Only that time he held me a little closer, his breath was warm against my face, and when he gazed into my eyes, I did not care that he was late.

"I do love you," Eddy said. "I'm just stupid."

We used to make love by candlelight.

Life is coming undone: my debt-load of an education, my shitty job and my boyfriend, even my clothes. The dream is ending and it was never even that good to begin with.

Susan Farrell

8. Your Partner.

What is the most significant event between you and your partner? What effect does this event have on you and/or the relationship?

Eddy:

Liz packed everything in less than fifteen minutes – the clothes, the gear, the food, the cameras, probably even the fucking souvenirs.

"Are you ready?" she said.

Interior.

Liz even packed my things. All the stuff was stacked and ready to go; she was standing by the door when I got in. There was a cup of coffee made and waiting for me. She seemed quiet, her eyes were glossy, but Dakota and his girl-friend were talking in the living room.

"They got here early," she said.

The relationship study kit was on the kitchen table.

"I guess we'll do that when we get back, eh," I said.

"Yeah."

And then she quoted something. Who knows, I wasn't listening.

Brangwen, Dakota's new girlfriend, was about twenty years old. The only thing we knew about her was that she wasn't Amber, the girl who had originally been included in this trip. Amber was nice; I liked her but no one else seemed to like her. Hell, I also liked Colette, that weird European girl Liz hung out with but no one seemed to like. Dakota met this girl at Starbucks.

The women sat in the back seat; my little brother Dave and his girlfriend were meeting us there.

Dakota was talkative, anything and everything got his attention: the new highway expansion, the Grapes-R-Us store and the breaking news of some politician who had been caught drinking. He knew I was going to ask Liz to marry me; his chatter was getting on my nerves but he just wouldn't shut the fuck up.

"How many burgers you want?" Liz's father asked me.

I was drinking a beer.

We visited her parents last summer; they wouldn't let us sleep together in the same room so Liz was in her old bedroom and I slept in the guest bedroom in the basement, which was okay – there was a big screen TV. Liz kept sneaking out of her room though and crawling into bed with me. She wasn't even looking for sex; it was more like she didn't want to be in her room.

Liz grew up in a two-storey house near the coke ovens at the defunct Sydney Steel plant; her father had a double garage in the backyard and a pool with a large deck. It reminded me of my old home in Halifax only we had a covered veranda and they had a porch. Her grandmother, recently widowed, had just moved in with her parents.

It was a family barbecue: her parents, her crazy grandmother, her cousin, Sharon and her husband. You could tell the cousin and her husband had been fighting all day.

The old woman stares.

"What does your father do?" Liz's father asked.

"He was in education," I said. "He's retired now."

"Right on, right on."

Liz and her cousin Sharon were inside with her mother; they were in the kitchen making a salad. The men were outside at the grill.

"What do you do?"

"I work in a warehouse," I said.

"Can't you do that around here?" he asked.

There are no jobs in Sydney.

Liz's old man flipped a burger on the grill. Fat dripped from the burgers and sizzled on the charcoals. A flame shot up through the grill and the old man gave a hearty laugh. His barbecue probably cost a month's rent for me; it was a good-looking barbecue. It was a good-looking house, some brick, a big veranda; his house was probably worth nothing because of the neighbourhood while the ugly houses in our area cost the price of a soul.

As we started eating at the table on the back deck, the grandmother started humming a tune. She was senile and on a waiting list to get into some sort of senior's facility. Everyone ignored her and continued eating. The father was talking about politics; something somewhere he didn't like.

"Shame you missed your Uncle Roy's funeral," the mother said to Liz. The mother glared at Liz like maybe missing a funeral was the worst crime in the world. We never had enough money for Liz to fly home for a funeral and besides, she didn't want to go.

Liz kept eating.

A damaged bird won't make it.

"Your uncle, my brother," the mother said, "was a good man. He thought the world of you."

The mother wanted a response, but Liz kept eating.

Cousin Sharon rolled her eyes and started laughing bitterly; she was Uncle Roy's kid. She was muttering beneath her breath, but I couldn't make out her words.

"Who did you vote for in the last election?" the father asked me suddenly. "Hmm?"

Liz and I didn't vote. The politicians are all lying arseholes. Not the kind of thing I wanted to say to Liz's father though, so I drank my beer, hoping the moment would disappear. No one wanted to talk about good old Roy and no one wanted to talk about good old politics. This was a fucking awesome trip.

The cousin's husband drank his beer and still said nothing. The grandmother was still humming. The whole time Liz's mother was still prattling on and on about good old Roy the lawyer who had four daughters and only one of them made it to the funeral. Cousin Sharon was still mumbling.

"Eddy and I think politics are private, Dad," Liz said.

"Yeah," I said.

The grandmother started muttering that she had to go to the bathroom. She got louder and louder, but everyone was still ignoring her. She was wearing one of those adult diapers.

"I travel a fair amount for business, myself," the father said.

I could buy a house here.

"More than usual now," the mother said. "Is the whore getting demanding?"

Suddenly, she was not talking about good old Roy anymore.

Everyone ignored that comment.

We ate in silence.

The British Columbia interior was different. The interior was four souls travelling to the guts of the world: the highway was empty, the trees went on for miles and the sky was a perfect blue – bright and pure. Not one single cloud.

You could smell the fresh mountain air before you were even out of the city. It was like the highway knew the Jeep was heading towards the desert of the interior: the blue skies above, the white cap on the mountains and the dip in the horizon where you knew the path to the interior was waiting for you. Everything was fresh and invigorating. You had to drive with the windows down just so you could get the full effect of the trip. You don't want to miss something that good. Especially when you don't know if you're ever going to get it again.

"What time is Dave arriving?" Liz asked.

"I'm not sure, has to talk to his girlfriend first," I said.

Midnight is quiet.

We were asleep in our sleeping bags on the shore. The sounds of loons and the water lapping against the shore woke me up, but Liz was still asleep. The campfire was already lit; Dave was sitting on a log staring outward at the lake.

"I think we got too drunk last night," Dave said.

"It's all just fun," I said. "We're on vacation."

Dave wasn't convinced, but he left to grab the thing to make coffee. I decided to go for a walk.

I don't know why; I wasn't really thinking about it. I mean, I know I was thinking about shit and stuff and just whatever. I was thinking about Liz but she never cared about that. She was the whole fucking reason I got up so fucking early and to do whatever the fuck it was I was doing.

Your one and only.

It was her. It was always her.

There was this tree; it almost had no leaves and branches. It was dying – the bark was all peeling and insects and creatures and whatever chewed it up. There were gnaw marks on two sides. The tree was on an incline looking down over the lake. The campsite wasn't visible though. Sometimes voices carried when there was no wind but exact words weren't decipherable. They were voices without words. I sat beneath the tree, I felt alone, and it felt good.

You think about what you did, young man.

So here you are. You finally did it. You're twenty-eight. You're a man. You got a job. You got a woman. You're off somewhere where the skies feel bigger and the horizon isn't geometric and shiny. You know you need some time alone. You know you need some time to think.

The only problem is you don't know what you're supposed to be thinking about. There are so many things other people tell you should be thinking about: they tell you what your concerns should be and what it takes to be a happy person but it's all sort of tongue-in-cheek.

No one tells you that sometimes you're going to like it when your best friend makes an ass of himself. No one tells you that there's going to be a moment when you hate yourself because you felt glad your mother finally died 'cause it was taking so long. No one tells you there's going to be a moment when you look at your girlfriend and think she's a royal-class bitch. No one tells you hatred can be so close to the surface. No one tells you it can make you so lonely.

Midnight.

I got back around midnight. The campsite was quiet except for the crackling – the fire was still going – it was cold. Dakota and Brangwen had gone off to the lake to go for a swim or a fuck. It was too dark to tell but it sounded like there was some special activity happening. Probably a little of each. I warmed my hands up, had a hot dog and a couple of s'mores and then crawled into my tent.

Wren was pretending to be asleep because she was so mad at me she couldn't bare to even look at me. She can't look at me when she's angry because she'll smile and she won't be able to *maintain* her anger. And sometimes, she wanted to maintain her anger. She was all stiff and kept turning away from me. You get used to that sort of thing after awhile so you make like nothing is wrong and you wait for it all to pass.

Wait. Wait.

Sometimes all you can do is wait.

Wait some more.

When you're young, you go through this phase where you don't want to get married, but you want someone to marry you. You want it, but you don't want the responsibility that goes with it. You want to be able to screw around and get as much ass as you can. But you also want this one woman who's going to redeem you somehow. There has to be the one woman who will make you give up the whores. But you never want to meet her early on in life.

Virgins.

"You're just like Saint Augustine," Liz said.

"Sweetheart, the last thing I am is a saint."

Saint Augustine. Who the hell is Saint Augustine? It was a weird thing for Liz to say – she's usually pretty perceptive. She's not even religious for God's sake, although she's always going on about how God always listens to her. She usually knows exactly how I am and what I'm thinking and feeling. She's got ESP.

Virgins with sexual experience.

"I'm not in the mood," she said.

Wren was sitting beneath these flower-covered trees. She looked pretty and soft, like a watercolour picture. Her hair was all tied back in a ponytail and she was reading a book (one that I got her). She was wearing her sunglasses and some short little white sundress. The flowers were surrounding her – they were white and pink and they smelled good.

No one else was around.

Sometimes when you get so nervous, you can't feel time. Time just passes, but for you there's nothing. It's like you're stuck in the *one moment* and that one moment goes on and on and on. Wren was laughing at me for a while before I even knew she saw me. *Apparently*, I was standing in front of her for a *long* time.

"Eddy? What is it?"

"Uh."

"Eddy?"

She was smiling and giggling.

Dakota should have written something for me.

"Eddy?"

"Should we barbecue for supper?"

Liz looked at me like I was lying. (ESP). She pulled her sunglasses off her face and stared at me. She shut the book.

"Yeah, sure. That sounds good."

She smiled.

When you get nervous and you back out, you like to leave the scene of the crime as soon as possible. There ain't too much sense in hanging around because that increases your chance of getting caught. You don't want that – especially when the person who's doing the catching is someone as smart as Liz.

But that day was different. It was hot and everything smelled like sand, burnt barbecue and tree sap – we were in the interior. That moment was why I wanted to be there. In the interior where there was no clutter. There comes a point in your life when you know you have to make some decisions and figure out what you're going to do and whether or not you're a boy or a man. There is a difference. And when you don't want to admit it – well, that means, you're still a boy. There was cold beer sitting in the wet dripping ice in the metal cooler under the tree right next to Liz.

Beer.

Grabbing an ice-cold beer and some potato chips, I sat in the shade beside her. She smelled like fresh soap and flowers. Her lips were wet with lemonade when I kissed her – I pulled out her ponytail and she giggled.

She was all in a knot about something. She leaned forward and squeezed my hand between both of her hands. Her voice had a certain urgency in it, like maybe she was telling me there was a fire in the house or I got fired or she was pregnant or something like that. I had to relive the conversation a couple of times to make sure I didn't miss anything. Maybe she just thinks that *men* can't talk about *relationships*. Liz sometimes thinks she's better than men cause she's so smart.

What the fuck?

"Yeah."

What the fuck?

"I can't believe you want to do a relationship study," Liz said.

Easy money.

"You and I. This has been on my mind for awhile."

Insert musical notes here.

You hear something like that and you think you've scored pretty damn fucking big. You came to the interior with a purpose and holy shit boy, she had the same fucking purpose. It's like you were meant to be together all along. It's like you lived your whole shitty miserable life to become the person who would give you this one great moment that would make sense of all the insanity. This moment made everything else make sense. If you weren't so damn cynical, you might even fucking believe in fate. You just never thought you'd end up with someone as beautiful as her. So beautiful.

You have the moment. You take it. Hesitation can be your worst enemy. It may get you once, or twice or even three times but after awhile, hesitation don't get you anymore, you get yourself. That's what my old man always told me: *you make or break yourself.* Then he'd have some more rum and say it again – *you make or break yourself* – in case no one was listening the first time around. And no one ever is. That's why you keep hesitating. When you can identify the hesitation, you can't use it as an excuse anymore. Cause you learn if you want to.

"Liz," I said. "I've been thinking, too."

Her eyes got shiny. Blue and glowing. Like melting ice in the spring. Her eyes are very round. Her lashes stuck together with the moisture. She tried to smile, but she bit her lower lip instead. (She always does that when she's nervous.) She wasn't wearing any makeup and she was still beautiful. Her face was slightly flushed with a pale rose colour.

She reached for her sunglasses, but I held her hand. She wasn't wearing any rings at all – not even her chunky gold graduate rings from the university – she usually wears those rings all the time. She had tan lines on her fingers from where she used to wear the rings. Her palms were sweaty. Her watch had stopped ticking. There was perspiration under the glass dome and the watch face was foggy. You just knew that meant you were going to have to get her a new one. Liz squeezed my hand tightly.

"What do you think of kids, Wren?" It had taken me all day to ask her. "What do you think of me and you – getting married – being a real family? With kids. What do you think, Wren?"

The sweat leaked out of her eyes and dripped down her cheek.

She asked for some time to think about it. Not exactly the way I imagined it.

I really fucked things up.

At last, relief.

"I can't believe you're finally out of the bathroom, man," Dakota says.

"Yeah, listen," I say. "I've been thinking about this whole relationship thing and I need to talk to Liz."

"I can't find her. She's not inside," Dakota said.

<u>Liz:</u>

Love crawled slowly into the tent, stumbled cautiously into the sleeping bag, and lay with me.

Midnight is for lovers.

It was midnight. Love was snuggled like a newborn child into the curve of my spine and love breathed deeply and contentedly. His chilled lips skimmed the nape of my neck and he whispered softly,

"I love you."

Shivering and a little wet, he felt like the first ice in winter – he must have fallen in the lake. He sighed. He nuzzled his face into my hair and then began to speak in a hushed voice about something – something about the black sky, the crescent moon, and the serenity of the lake. He smelled like whiskey.

"I love you," he whispered again. His voice was low and husky and there was a dreamy tone in his words. Each word lasted a moment and carried a small pang from my receiving ears down down down into my heart. Three small beats. Tump. Tump. Tump.

I love you.

And I suddenly knew two things: that this was the absolute truth for Eddy, and that he was the closest I would ever come to love. This was love. This was my love. His voice was deep and low and caused a stir in my heart and I was so very close to loving him. Eddy.

When he talks and expresses himself, his voice slows down and I tingle all over. Through thick and through thin, through beauty, oddities, trivia and mundane pathos, he has been my everything. My Eddy.

The never-ending gaze of his deep blue eyes.

Of everyone I have ever been with, he has meant the most. Through my needy infatuation with Adam and any other misgiving I may have ever had, Eddy is the *one*. He is my most honest partner. And after all that, the only thing I can say about him is that I nearly love him. I am close to loving him. Perhaps that is a feat. Perhaps it is love but I have lost the ability to know it. When I see my life before me – in images of black and images of white – I think that this man, this love, is my most miraculous feat.

Despite his vocal desire to have oral sex with everyone and despite his inability to say the word "penis" and despite his overuse of the word "fuck" and his misuse of the word "get," he has been the most honest. He has never lied to me. He will be special in a way that he will not understand. Close only counts in horseshoes and hand grenades. But in the end, we will both know that *close* doesn't count in love.

The voices were so loud.

"Where do you see yourself in five years?" Dakota asked. We were sitting on the beach watching the sunset. The conversation began innocently. At some point, the questions about the weather and the hockey scores had changed. We were no longer prattling about the party last weekend and the contemporary restaurant on the corner and Dave's new fox terrier. We were talking about things of substance.

Dakota's voice was formal and unyielding when he asked it and his eyes were clouded with dubiousness. He was frozen with his black eyes gazing into the pit of the fire. The flames came in waves, making his face appear dark then light; it was difficult to see him.

The current girlfriend was making s'mores. Dave was poking the fire with a stick. Eddy and I, seated together, were quiet.

Our faces had lost the subtle laughing lines. We were austere and sun burnt in the fervent glow of the campfire. The questions were probing, even accusatory.

Picket fences.

Dakota was so stiff, he seemed unreal.

Finally, his chest heaved, and through the flames, I could see him lean forward and as sweat dribbled across his brow, he seemed to be looking only at me.

"Five years ago, I never thought I'd be here."

Baby turtles wriggling toward the ocean.

Eddy squirmed like a worm on wet pavement. He rubbed his nose until the flesh was chafed. He adjusted his ball cap and tried to chortle. But his mouth could not hold the shape of the smile and it all fell apart. He yanked a beer from the cooler instead. His hands were trembling; as they knotted about the familiarity of the beer bottle; his fingers were still imprecise.

"Yeah, if you had asked me five years ago," Dakota said, "where I thought I'd be, what I thought I'd be doing, that sort of thing. That sort of life question. I just never would have said this, you know?"

"I thought I'd have kids by now," Eddy said.

If only there had been signs earlier.

The bottle slipped from Eddy's hand. Snatching at it as it dropped through the air, he caught it just before it smashed against the beach rocks. His hands were still shaking. They couldn't squeeze. He had to hold the bottle with both hands.

"Where's the pot?" Brangwen asked.

No one answered her.

She must have gotten up to find some. I don't remember her leaving but she never returned. I don't remember when I noticed she wasn't there.

I love you.

The flames from the fire seemed to crackle within my ears. The night was golden and primitive – I was waiting for the primordial drives to kick in. Sometimes it was hard to hear Dakota. It was the loudest fire I had ever heard. It reminded me of nothing.

Dakota didn't seem surprised when Brangwen did not return. Perhaps he never noticed she had left – he never paid her much attention and she seemed disinterested in our philosophic conversation. She was only young, it didn't matter, she was at the age where she wanted to make all of our mistakes because that's her right. She didn't want to learn from us; she wanted to repeat us. Again and again.

At any rate, she was gone and Dakota was unmoved by her lack of devotion and adoration. The astounding rigidity of his face remained intact. He stuck a marshmallow on the end of his kabob stick and plunged it into the flames.

The marshmallow was still chunky and white. It swerved throughout the flames. Eddy was mesmerized by this sight; his eyes followed the marshmallow's every dive and curve.

"My high school reunion was last year. I didn't go. Do you want to hear why I didn't go? Liz?"

When I heard him call my name, I was stunned. There was no reaction from Eddy – like perhaps he never even heard the word mentioned. But Eddy was so centralized on the marshmallow; he was oblivious of anything else. He gulped down his beer and then automatically, his shaking hands reached over and grabbed another bottle from the cooler. He gashed open the palm of his hand when he unscrewed the top. He didn't seem to notice.

Eddy was upset, but I couldn't give him an answer to that haphazard proposal.

Dakota has only ever called me by name once.

Dakota.

The blinds were drawn. A bright golden sun, still nothing visible through the blinds on our tiny basement window. We were lying on the floor in piles of pillows.

Eddy had gone away for the weekend with his brother; they had gone to see their father for some reason. Dakota arrived half an hour after Eddy left. He carried a bottle of wine in one hand and a book of Lord Byron's poetry in the other.

There was no pretence.

We fucked.

And as we lay in the piles of pillows afterwards, he refused to look at me. He lay with his back to me. His shoulder was raised high to create the sense of a wall.

"I love you, Liz," he said.

I said nothing.

Dakota.

It was a mistake. Everything I do is just one mistake after another.

"I didn't go to my high school reunion because I'm still in school. I'm twenty-eight years old and I'm still in school. I've never left school," Dakota said. "I am still in school."

High school is the best time of your life.

"I didn't have my ten-year reunion yet," Dave said. "It hasn't been ten years."

No one cared.

Eddy doesn't ever mention his insecurities about Dakota and me because he doesn't want an answer. He doesn't want me to lie, but he doesn't want the truth. Through the process of elimination, Eddy wants nothing. He thinks he wants what people tell him he should want and people always tell other people that they want the truth.

We knew he was talking to me. Dakota never has this type of conversation with Eddy – it's too impassioned. Eddy was shivering so I put a sweater over his shoulders. When I squeezed him, he kissed me softly under my chin. I opened a beer before I answered Dakota.

"What can I say?"

Dakota laughed so quietly that it was barely audible, but it was bitter. His face was strong and tense – his eyes were dead flat. He took a long, deep breath and gazed into the flames with far away eyes and I could hear his voice.

I love you.

The marshmallow on the end of Dakota's kabob was aflame. Eddy started muttering and cursing. He yanked Dakota's arm to pull the marshmallow from the flames, but it was completely charred within seconds. The entire marshmallow was black and crusty – little flakes chipped off like a case of bad dandruff. Sweat dripped from Eddy's brow – I passed him another marshmallow from the bag.

I want to hold your hand.

Dakota let his hair fall loose. The silky black strands shone in the firelight. His hair was just past his shoulders. He stared at me through the flames.

"I didn't want to be a number, another statistic. I didn't want to be unemployed – you know how everybody talks. It's like I was supposed to fail before I ever started."

He laughed again.

"I guess it backfired, eh?"

There was nothing to say. There was nothing to do. I could see the muscles tightening in Dakota's jaw and neck – he was in turmoil. Eddy was shaking. What could I say? Nothing. I drank my beer.

"Thus the whirligig of time brings in his revenges," Dakota quoted. "Shakespeare."

Eddy shut his eyes.

The three of us slept around the fire that night. I was the last one to fall asleep but the first one to lie down and close my eyes. My position was predetermined – there was nothing left for me in that conversation. In an ideal world, I could have said anything, but I'm not one of those people who live in an ideal world. Eddy drank himself to sleep.

Eddy sang Rolling Stones tunes, the same ones and the same choruses, over and over again. He doesn't know too many songs and the ones that he does know, he doesn't know all the words.

"I know the memorable lines," he said.

On bended knee.

Eddy always talked about sunsets. When we first started dating, we used to get coffee and drive to the harbourfront and watch the sailboats dock and enjoy the colours of the sunset. Eddy said sunset had always been his favourite colour and he desperately wanted a painting of a sunset for above the sofa. We had to trudge through every flea market and craft fair seeking out the right sunset painting. He had a vision in his head and he had to be true to that vision. We couldn't just get any sunset.

Spiralling wisps of coffee vapours.

Dakota was making coffee. He fixed a cup for me and we drank in total silence. Silence can be misinterpreted though – was he trying to cause a rift between Eddy and me? Or was he finally letting go of this idea that I was his one and only? As he prepared my cup, I accepted it and maintained the silence. I couldn't afford to engage conversation and have it go in a direction I couldn't control.

Eddy tells Dakota everything.

Brangwen went for a swim.

The coffee warmed the cold tip of my nose and the smell reminded me of everything good in my life. Fresh coffee. Fresh life. The coffee was full bodied and intense and it felt earthy and thick like the trees all about us. Dakota sipped his coffee and smiled. I was living on borrowed time.

I can't have kids. I can't have kids. I can't have kids.

9. Future expectations.

Where do you envision this relationship going?

<u>Liz:</u>

If Eddy thinks I'm so beautiful then he can have pictures of my body; that's all he wants anyway. Take the pictures with you to the bathroom. I'm better than the Sears catalogue. What an accomplishment. I've done so much. Wank away.

It's just oral sex.

Fucker.

Your father goes away for "business."

What is this shitty beer?

It will be our little secret.

The cheap steak knife is broken. Cheap shit from the dollar store. How can you even manufacture a knife for a buck? Is that even possible? Somewhere there's a child being forced into child labour because I needed a fucking steak knife for a dollar that broke. I ruined a child's life for a steak knife. I ruined a child. I am a ruined child.

My student loan is $56,000? $84,000? $110,000?

Where am I supposed to stick these pictures? I need to stick these pictures somewhere. I need to fix everything.

If only there had been signs earlier.

People say they sell their soul but they don't really because you don't get any money for a soul. But I can sell my body. Maybe then I could finally pay off that phantasm of a student loan; they don't even know the correct amount. Can I get a get a discount for improper paperwork?

"Eddy doesn't even know why he's with you."

It's going to start raining. It's going to start raining and I'm naked and outside. The neighbours have gone away. I think. I think.

I love you.

I have nothing.

The eyes never lie.

I have a beautiful body that can't reproduce.

A deer caught in headlights. A deer caught in headlights. A deer caught in headlights. A deer caught in headlights. A deer caught in headlights. A deer caught in headlights. A deer caught in headlights. A deer caught in headlights. A deer caught in headlights. A deer caught in headlights. A deer caught in headlights. A deer caught in headlights.

Eddy:

So, a relationship study would be easier if the questions were like multiple choice or something. When everything you're doing is a blank page, what the hell are you supposed to do? What are you supposed to say? Where are you supposed to go? What are you supposed to do? Where do you even start? When you have too much, you can't do dick all.

"You see Liz yet?"

"She's just answering the survey somewhere," Dakota says as he goes into the bathroom. "Have a beer and chill, we'll find her in a minute. Do your last question."

I know why she'd take the shitty beer.

Liz can be bitchy.

Menstruation.

So it's a *female* thing and she wants to *talk* about it cause its part of her and sometimes, she just has to make reference to it and cause I'm *the boyfriend,* I just have to understand. *What's she supposed to do? Pretend like she doesn't have one?* Love her, love the menstruation. What are we going to talk about? Blood and pain? And what the fuck am I going to contribute to this conversation? I'm more than willing to fully and completely admit – I don't need to experience "just one period" to know I don't want one.

The feeling is, as Liz would say, *innate.* And why? 'Cause I ain't *the guy with the good attitude toward menstruation.* I ain't got nothing against it – some things are natural but that don't make them works of art to be discussed by the general public. I respect her menstruation. It's all part of being a woman.

Bodily functions.

Of or affecting the human body or physical nature.

I'm all for bodily functions: power to the bodily functions. They offer relief of all kinds – you got excess, you shit, you're sick, you puke, you're horny and you got lots of options. That's the beauty of bodily functions. I'm glad Liz menstruates – she can have kids and all that female stuff that goes with it, but why do I have to hear about it? It's not like I tell her about urine.

Urine stories.

Dakota takes over the bathroom. The whole time he's in there, he's spewing poetry and philosophy and all sorts of shit. As far as I can figure out, that's why he's a poet and I'm just a guy who makes tampons for a living. I can look at it that way or I can look at it this way: I can afford to buy him dinner. He's got useless degrees and no job capacity – compared to him I make a fucking fortune. He used to say that at least he'd get all the better chicks, but then Liz came along and killed that little theory.

"Hey, white boy."

It's all how you look it.

The eyes never lie.

As Dakota exits the bathroom, he looks at me – only I notice he's not looking me in the eye. I realize there's an overwhelming chance he took a shot at my insecure woman after I told her about the landlord's girlfriend. That's probably why she hesitated when I asked her to get married. What do I do with this information? Do I need to know? Maybe it didn't happen.

"What are you looking at me like that for?" Dakota says. "What's wrong?"

I don't want to know. I want to tell Liz I'm sorry, Dakota can get a real girlfriend and life will go on like it's supposed to go on. I don't want to know.

"What?" he says again. "Just finish the survey, man. You're almost done."

"Yeah."

"Just what are these individuals trying to accomplish anyway?" Dakota says as he cracks open another beer. "People have brains and brains are thinking organs."

People don't care enough anymore. It's all the same on TV and we're letting our young people be tainted with this poisoned geist that has permeated the current paradigm. People don't even know who Hegel is. Let's just all watch soap operas. It's not like we need to participate in our own lives. Liz would like that.

Half the time, he's talking so fast, I don't even know what he's trying to express and when he drinks like now, he keeps changing the subjects so quickly that I can't follow. Liz's name was undeniable though.

"You know she's my girlfriend, right?" I say.

"Man, you cheated on her," he says. "You told her about it and then you asked her to marry you."

"People fuck up," I say. "People make mistakes. That's life. We're supposed to be helping each other out here."

Sipping on his beer, he's quiet for a moment.

"Eddy," he mutters.

"Fuck off, man," I say. Don't say it. I don't want to hear it.

"I'll help you find her," he says.

"It doesn't matter anyway – it's only the end for my little world."

Smile and nod. Smile and nod. Smile and nod. Smile and nod. Smile and nod. Smile and nod. Smile and nod. Smile and nod. Smile and nod. Smile and nod. Smile and nod. Smile and nod.

Now is not the time to explode into a jealous rage. Now is the time to find Liz and make sure it's not too late. I don't want to know. Hatred is an all-consuming passion I don't ever want to know. I saw Brad. I don't ever want to be that kind of man.

Supposed to be.

I only agreed to do the relationship survey because it was a nice lump of money for what seemed like nothing. I just wanted some extra cash on hand so I could get Liz a ring. I can get her a ring, but I want to get her a real ring.

There should be an asset on her finger.

10. Other comments.

Please express any other comments you might have regarding your relationship.

Liz:

Eddy:

As I open the basement apartment, my ears go all funny like I'm walking under water. It's hard to breathe. I can hear Dakota talking to me but I can't really make him out, it's like his voice is far away. He sort of stands in my way, blocking my view of the backyard so I can't exit the basement entrance. He doesn't look sarcastic like he normally does; he looks like the Dakota from Nova Scotia. His jaw is clenched tightly.

Dakota's lips are moving:

"Eddy, just go back inside."

He had a bad experience.

A stack of pictures, all nude shots of Liz's body, is stuck to the back entrance way with one of our cheap dollar-store knives. The knife is broken, but the blade still manages to hold the pictures securely. The pictures feel rubbery.

A little note attached reads,

Sell these for cash.

And I'm thinking, dear God, let her be so pissed angry that she took all these naked pictures of herself and just left me in a fit of rage because I'm an asshole. I deserve that. Liz was never good with expressing her anger; the relationship study helped her express anger. Dear God. Let her be with Nina, or that Colette. Her friends came and got her and she's mad.

Dakota's lips are moving,

"Hey, John, can I get your assistance?"

Asshole.

The older couple from the upstairs apartment are standing in their entrance. They step into the backyard. They see me in the basement entrance but they look away; their eyes are glossy too. The man uses his cell phone.

A damaged bird won't make it.

Dakota's arm brushes against me,

"Eddy, go back inside."

A deer caught in headlights. A deer caught in headlights. A deer caught in headlights. A deer caught in headlights. A deer caught in headlights. A deer caught in headlights. A deer caught in headlights. A deer caught in headlights. A deer caught in headlights.

Looking over Dakota's shoulder, a little to the left, I see Liz. She's just lying there, on the grass, beneath the trees. Liz.

Liz.

Her body stained red.